"You're so ...
And his li...

It was the last thing she had expected from this man, and her mouth parted in a gasp of surprise, allowing him to deepen the kiss, to go further, deeper, into the moist recesses.

She had melted at his first touch, felt pleasure at the intimacy of his kiss as he continued the slow drudging movement, curving her body into the hardness of his, his hands moving restlessly from her thigh to her breasts.

The kiss might have gone on forever, might have become more than a kiss, with both of them caught up in the breathless moment of passion. But the sound of a gasp from the doorway had them pulling apart to see Rita Hammond looking at them in horror.

CAROLE MORTIMER
is also the author of these

Harlequin Presents

CAROLE MORTIMER

lifelong affair

Harlequin Books

TORONTO • NEW YORK • LONDON
AMSTERDAM • PARIS • SYDNEY • HAMBURG
STOCKHOLM • ATHENS • TOKYO • MILAN

For
John and Matthew

———————————◆—◆—◆———————————

Harlequin Presents first edition September 1983
ISBN 0-373-10627-0

Original hardcover edition published in 1983
by Mills & Boon Limited

CHAPTER ONE

'I KNOW you've been having an affair with my husband! I've known about it for weeks now. And if you want him you can have him. I don't even like him any more!'

Morgan watched in horror as the bitterly angry woman let loose that tirade, her mouth twisting in derisive humour as the words became ones of bravado, laughing openly as the woman took off her wedding ring and threw it at her.

'Okay, cut—that's a take. Morgan, you're becoming so convincing as the superbitch that I'm beginning to wonder about you,' Jerry, the director, drawled dryly.

Morgan's laughter had faded at the word 'cut'. She had played this scene half a dozen times today already, and each time she became more disgusted with the way her character in this weekly soap-opera was developing.

Originally she had been signed for a three-month contract only, but the character of Mary-Beth Barker had become so popular with the public that she had signed a contract for another season. The character of Mary-Beth was so against her own nature that she wasn't sure she wanted to negotiate another one. She had certainly had plenty of other offers the last six-months!

'Don't wonder, Jerry,' she advised wearily. 'It will be for nothing.' She came off the set, her hair long and gleaming, the colour of copper, a dark shadow over her sparkling green eyes, her lashes long and silky, her nose small and pert, her mouth wide and inviting, coloured with a brighter lip-gloss than she usually

7

wore, the blusher on her creamy cheeks darker too, for the cameras. Her green dress was thin and silky, very provocatively styled, part of Mary-Beth's wardrobe; her own taste tended to run to the casual and comfortable rather than fashionable. 'I'm nothing like Mary-Beth.' She stood next to him, a frown marring her smooth brow. 'In fact, I don't like where she's going at all. So far I've—*she's*—blackmailed her stepfather for his attraction to her, told her mother about it anyway, almost wrecked her sister's marriage, and now she's had an affair with a married man simply because his wife once slighted her at a party. What sort of woman is she!' she grimaced, running a hand through her perfectly smooth and shining hair, instantly ruffling it into disorder.

'Beautiful,' Jerry leered lasciviously.

'And evil,' she said disgustedly.

'You bet,' he nodded with a grin.

'You wouldn't sound so happy about it if she'd decided to get her claws into you!' Morgan raised copper-brown brows at him.

The director shrugged. 'The excitement might be worth it. When you've been married to the same woman for fifteen years that's a quality that seems to be missing.'

Morgan smiled, her own naturally bright and friendly smile, the character of Mary-Beth discarded as soon as the scene ended. 'I'll mention that to Alyson when I see her next,' she teased, knowing Jerry had been happily married from the moment he and Alyson had been pronounced husband and wife.

'She'd kill me,' he grimaced. 'And you're supposed to like Mary-Beth if no one else does. After all, she pays your rent.'

She knew that, but it didn't make the public reaction to her personally any easier to accept. Soap-operas were entertaining, and there were half a dozen of them made at this Los Angeles studio alone, but until she actually appeared in *Power Trap* herself she hadn't realised that the viewing public really believed the characters existed. A lot of men admired the character of Mary-Beth, liked the danger she emitted, but normally women reacted in a hostile manner, treating her like an adversary, watching their husbands closely whenever she was about. Even some of her so-called friends had become a little wary of her, sure that she couldn't have developed the character of Mary-Beth the way she had if there weren't some of the man-eating bitch really inside the straight-speaking Morgan McKay.

Over the months she had hardened herself against the insulting comments she received whenever she went out, although it didn't stop it hurting any less. When the new series came out in the fall her reputation—or rather, Mary-Beth's—would be damaged irrevocably.

She went back to her dressing-room, switching on the television for relaxation as she changed into her own denims and orange silk blouse, tall and slender, dulling the make-up down to be less dramatic, brushing her hair free of lacquer and feeling it swing easily past her shoulders in its normal copper straightness.

'You were great today!' Sam Walters came into the room after a brief knock, and kissed her lingeringly on the mouth.

Morgan returned his kiss, glad to see him. Sam played her brother-in-law in *Power Trap*, and the two of them had been seeing each other out of work for the last four months. Tall and blond, with the body of an ex-footballer, Sam had to be every woman's ideal, his easygoing nature and strong sense of humour merely a bonus.

'Thanks,' she smiled up at him, her arms about his

neck as he held her close. 'How about going to your beach-house tonight?'

'Sounds good,' he nodded. 'Barbecue dinner?'

'Lovely,' she agreed, turning to pick up her purse.

'—and it's now known that Glenna McKay and her husband Mark Hammond were on the aircraft that crashed late last night on its way from London to Los Angeles. There are thought to be no survivors from the crash, now believed to have been caused by engine failure.' The television newsreader then went on to another topic of news.

But for Morgan the world seemed to have stopped. Glenna and Mark . . .! It couldn't be, there must have been some mistake. And yet Glenna had insisted she wanted the baby born in the States, and she was in her seventh month now. God, the baby too . . . No——!

'Steady, honey!' she didn't realise she had spoken out loud until Sam answered her, sitting her down in one of the plush armchairs in the room.

'Sam, did you hear—Did she say——'

'Yes,' he confirmed heavily, frowning his concern of her paper-white face. 'I heard it too, Morgan.'

'My God—Glenna!' she choked, too shocked to cry yet, too numbed by the horror of hearing on the television of her own sister's possible death. Possible . . .! Who was she kidding, there were hardly ever survivors from those sort of disasters. Her parents! They would have to be told——

'We'll call them in a minute,' Sam soothed as she once again spoke out loud without being aware of it, kneeling beside her to comfort her in her distress.

Glenna. Her elder by two years, her fiery hair matching her equally fiery nature—she couldn't possibly be dead! Air crashes happened on television, to other people, other families, they didn't happen to young fun-loving couples like Glenna and Mark, certainly not to *unborn* babies!

She couldn't believe this was happening, that her sister could actually have been on the plane that had crashed late last night. She had heard the first reports of it early this morning, had felt saddened for the families of the people on the plane, never dreaming that she would be one of them!

Glenna had been a successful actress herself until two years ago she had married Mark Hammond, an English businessman she had met and fallen in love with in Florida. The marriage had been far from idyllic—had been? Heavens, already she was talking in the past tense, as if she accepted that Glenna and Mark were dead.

She and Glenna had been born and brought up in the States, had always lived here apart from a few holidays abroad, and having to give up her career as a successful actress to go and live in England with her husband had not been something Glenna accepted without a fight. And she had continued to fight, had hated living with her in-laws at the Hammond house in southern England. The Hammonds were almost part of the aristocracy, something Glenna's mother-in-law had taken great pains to point out to Glenna any opportunity she could. Morgan could just imagine how her sister had reacted to that! In fact, she knew how Glenna had reacted to it; she had spent hours talking to her sister long-distance—calls her sister had made, claiming the Hammonds could more than afford the telephone bill. She knew from those calls that Glenna had been far from happy, had longed for her career and the physical, if not emotional, freedom she had always had in the States. The Hammonds had put restrictions on her behaviour and her social life, restrictions Mark had seemed happy to accept for his wife.

The one stipulation Glenna had made when she had had her pregnancy confirmed five months ago had been that the baby be born at her home and not Mark's. In the face of strong family opposition, mainly Rita Hammond's, Mark had finally agreed, and the two of them had flown to their deaths.

'I have to call my parents,' said Morgan in short jerky gasps. 'If they should hear the news in the same way . . .!'

'They probably already have,' Sam soothed.

Oh God, this was a nightmare! Her mother had probably collapsed, her father would be bottling his emotions inside him as usual. He wasn't a man who found it easy to show his love, although she and Glenna had never doubted his love for his family. But this was something no one had expected in their wildest nightmares!

'I have to get home——'

'I'll drive you,' Sam instantly offered as she stood up agitatedly.

'My parents' home,' she pointed out. 'They're going to need me.'

'I'll still drive you,' he insisted.

'You still have a scene to shoot this evening,' she reminded him calmly, thinking logically despite the panicked racing of her brain. 'Jerry was only complaining yesterday that we're behind schedule.'

Sam shrugged. 'So we finish shooting mid-September instead of the end of August,' he dismissed. 'The network can't complain, not with the ratings we're getting. I hear we're very popular with the English audience. Hell, what am I going on like this for?' he muttered. 'What do you care about the reaction of the English audience at a time like this! I'll just go and tell Jerry we're leaving.' He gently touched her cheek before going to talk to their director.

Morgan stood in numbed silence waiting for him to return. Sam was wrong about her not caring about what the English audience thought of the show. A couple of months ago Glenna had telephoned her in a great state of agitation, crying and muttering what a bitch her mother-in-law was. Apparently Rita Hammond had taken great delight in the fact that Glenna's sister should be appearing in something so lowly as a soap-opera, had taken every opportunity she could to be derogative about *Power Trap* and Morgan's part in it. Normally Glenna would have been unmoved by such taunts, but her pregnancy had made her more susceptible to showing emotion, and she had been very distraught.

Jerry himself came into the room just then, his weatherbeaten face creased into lines of sadness. 'Hell, Morgan, Sam just told me.' He grasped her forearms, frowning down at her. 'That's a hell of a thing to hear on the television,' he growled.

'Yes.' She was still too numb to respond to the sincerity of his regret.

'I was fond of Glenna,' he continued softly. 'She and I worked together a couple of years ago, before she married her stuffed shirt,' he grimaced. 'We're all going to miss her.'

Morgan swallowed hard, as nausea started to rise within her, the numbness leaving her at Jerry's way of talking about her sister as if she no longer existed. 'Excuse me,' she muttered, pushing past him to run into the wash-room, waves of nausea racking her body as the full horror of her beautiful and fiery sister dying in such a horrendous way struck her. Glenna had always been too busy in her life to think of death, and Morgan certainly doubted she ever expected it to happen in such a violent way. None of them had.

'All right?' Jerry was helping her wash her face in cold water when Sam came back into the room.

'Better,' she nodded, swallowing the nausea down. She had to pull herself together, had to be strong for her parents' sake, her strong attorney father, her homemaking mother. They were going to be devastated. 'I'll have to pick up some things from my apartment,' she told Sam as he drove her.

'Sure,' he agreed easily, not intruding on her private thoughts as she lapsed into silence.

Strangely her apartment still looked the same as when she had left it early this morning, the same casual untidiness that she liked, the galley kitchen, scatter cushions placed on her corner unit in the lounge, a cup still standing on the dining-room table from where she had had breakfast, plants arranged about the whole apartment, one of her weaknesses, her other one being the Walt Disney posters in her bedroom. She knew that the general public, after her portrayal of Mary-Beth, would never believe her liking for all things Disney, but it had remained with her from a trip to Disneyland when she was a child. A trip both she and Glenna had loved. Oh God, Glenna . . .!

All this was a terrible dream, one that she couldn't believe until someone could tell her it was true, someone who really knew. After all, the news item could have been wrong; maybe Glenna and Mark hadn't been on that flight, maybe they should have been but something had prevented them making it, maybe——

The telephone at her bedside began ringing, and she snatched up the receiver, feeling her heart plummet at the sound of her mother's voice, a strangely strong voice, her mother seeming filled with a determination that wasn't a normal facet of her nature, their father the strong one.

'You've heard, Morgan?' she asked briskly.

'Yes,' her voice caught huskily. 'It was on the television just now.'

Her mother sighed. 'I wonder if they realise how cruel they can be,' she said waspishly, a small black-haired woman of fifty, filled with a restless energy that put younger women to shame. 'Alex Hammond called us a short time ago, so at least we didn't hear that way.'

Alex Hammond. A picture of a tall dark-haired man with a remote manner, autocratic features; piercing grey eyes, aquiline nose, thinned lips, determined jaw, and a lithe athletic body came to mind. Mark's brother, the elder by eight years at thirty-eight, he ran the family business like a well-oiled cog, had little time for the rest of the human race, having no wife and apparently no steady woman in his life either. Morgan had met him only once, at the wedding two years ago, and she hadn't liked him, not his arrogance or his haughtiness.

'I would have telephoned you at the studio,' her mother continued, her voice showing some sign of strain now. 'But I've been busy with—Your father collapsed, Morgan,' her voice broke, still a little trembly as she continued. 'He answered the telephone to Mr Hammond, and he seemed all right at the time. Then he just—he's had a heart attack!'

This was worse than a nightmare, the whole world was going crazy! 'I—Is he——'

'He's in hospital, but his condition has stabilised,' her mother hastily assured her. 'The doctors are sure he's going to be all right.'

'I'm coming home——'

'No! Morgan, I told Alex Hammond we would be coming to you—that was before your father collapsed, of course. He said he would get in touch again when he knew anything more than that Glenna and Mark were on the plane.' The line went silent for several minutes, as her mother fought for control. 'He was expecting to know more later today.'

Alex Hammond would be the type of man who demanded, not asked for, that information. And he had such a presence of authority that he would get the answers too!

'I'd rather come home. Mr Hammond will realise I'm there when he gets no answer here.'

'I'm not at home, Morgan,' her mother told her softly. 'I'm going to stay at the hospital with your father tonight.'

'Are you sure there's no danger?' Morgan asked sharply, wondering if her mother was telling her everything.

'The doctors assure me there isn't,' she was hastily assured. 'But I'd rather be with him tonight. Please stay in Los Angeles and wait for Mr Hammond to contact you. I'd hate for us to miss his call.'

Her mother was right, she knew she was, and yet she felt she should go to her father. But if Alex Hammond should telephone while she was in transit ....! 'I'll wait, Mom,' she said softly. 'And I'll call you at the hospital as soon as I know anything.' There was only one hospital in the small California town her parents lived in. 'Give Dad my love.'

'I will, dear. And don't worry, things could still be all right with Glenna and Mark.'

She couldn't move after putting down the receiver. Her mother was being optimistic, and they both knew it. Glenna was going to be dead, Mark too, and their poor little baby that hadn't even begun to live. And no matter how light her mother made of the heart attack she knew her father was gravely ill.

'I thought I heard the telephone——'

With a strangled cry she turned and flung herself into Sam's waiting arms, a dam seeming to burst as she sobbed it all out to him, finding comfort in his lean strength as he led her back to the lounge, holding her close against his chest as she sat close beside him on the corner unit.

'She was so beautiful, Sam,' she choked, her tears

having wet his shirt front. 'I can't believe she's dead—and in that way. No wonder Dad took it so hard,' she shuddered.

'I know, honey. I know,' he soothed, smoothing back her hair with a gentle hand, surprisingly so considering their size and strength. Tall and slender as she was, Sam made her feel cherished and cared for, his manners were always without fault, never too forward, but always friendly.

'You never met Glenna, did you?' she mumbled into his shirt.

'I've seen her in the movies. She was beautiful,' he acknowledged. 'Very like you.'

Again they were talking in the past tense, and it was with a sense of deep pain that she realised she would probably never see her sister again. Of a similar age, the two of them had always been very close, had shared friends and clothes during their teenage years, continuing to keep those same friends as the years passed. Everyone was going to be heartbroken when they learnt the fiery-haired Glenna was no longer with them.

'Everyone loved her, Sam,' she continued huskily. 'She was so much fun, so—so full of life!' Her voice broke over the last.

Everyone *had* loved Glenna—except the Hammonds. Glenna and Mark had a private wing in the Hammond house, the widowed Rita Hammond and her bachelor son occupying the other wing, while the married daughter Janet lived several miles away with her husband and two daughters. Rita Hammond and her daughter Janet had shown their disapproval of Mark marrying an American actress from the first; the formidable Alex Hammond had been indifferent. Mark was a charming rogue, very dark and handsome, but he was no match for the rest of his family, resisting all Glenna's efforts to persuade him to move to America, claiming that he had to stay in England to work in the family firm, and also claiming it was unnecessary to have a house of their own when the family house was so big.

Living with her in-laws wouldn't suit Morgan, and she knew that it hadn't suited Glenna, although in the beginning she had been too much in love to object to anything Mark decided. Her one stubborn bid for freedom, that of having her baby born in the States, seemed to have caused their deaths.

Morgan pulled herself together with effort; she was not one to allow emotional trauma to take her to the hysterical stage. 'You should be getting back, Sam,' she told him in a firm voice. 'I shall be all right now, and you do have that scene to finish.'

'Jerry told me to stay with you.'

'But I don't need "being with"!' She sounded brittle, highly strung, knowing she needed to be alone for a while to come to terms with her loss. She deeply appreciated Sam's gentle care, but no amount of talking was going to help her through the next few hours as she waited for Alex Hammond's call. 'Really, Sam,' she insisted as he made to protest. 'I need time to—accept.'

'Time alone,' he nodded understandingly, having lost his young wife in an automobile accident four years ago when they had only been married a year. He stood up, tall and assuring. 'If you need me, any time day or night, just call, hmm?' He framed her face tenderly with his large capable hands.

She appreciated his lack of argument, knowing she didn't have the strength to fight him if he insisted on staying. 'Thank you,' she blinked back the tears. 'Until I get this call from Alex Hammond my hands are tied. I can't go to England where the crash happened, and I can't go to Dad either.'

Sam bent and kissed her lightly on the lips. 'I'm sure he won't be long.'

But the evening passed, and then the night-time hours, and still Alex Hammond hadn't called her. Morgan paced the room most of the night, the time dragging slowly, until finally in desperation she telephoned the Hammonds' house herself. She wasn't proud, and if they wouldn't come to her then she would go to them.

It took some time to convince Symonds, the Hammond butler, that she really was Glenna's sister and not a reporter trying to get a story. It seemed the Hammond telephone hadn't stopped ringing since the news broke.

'Mrs Hammond has been sedated and is in her bedroom,' she was informed in a haughty voice, and for a moment it took her back that the Mrs Hammond he was talking about was Rita and not Glenna. 'Mrs Fairchild,' he spoke of Mark's married sister, 'is at home with her own family.'

'And Mr Hammond?' she asked breathlessly, not giving a damn where Rita and Janet were, not having taken to either of them at the wedding. Mother and daughter were too much alike, both narrow-minded and condescending, believing all actresses to be promiscuous sirens.

'Mr Hammond isn't at home,' she was told.

'Not there?' she frowned.

'No, miss,' the man sounded affronted that she should dare to question his statement, 'he left the house several hours ago.'

'To go where?' she demanded impatiently.

'I wouldn't know, Miss McKay.' Symonds sounded surprised by such a question. 'Mr Hammond doesn't inform me of his movements.'

'Then in the circumstances he damn well should!' Morgan slammed the receiver down, too angry to question more.

Damn the man! Where could Alex Hammond have

disappeared to, and apparently without telling anyone where he was going? No doubt Rita Hammond knew of her son's whereabouts, but it seemed she was taking the joint deaths as badly as Morgan's father had. From what she had been able to tell, Mark was the favourite son, a late edition to the family who had been cossetted by all around him. Rita Hammond would have felt his death severely.

But all this didn't change the fact that Alex Hammond had promised to call, that she had held off calling the hospital about her father in case she missed that call, and now he had disappeared. She had been relying on his authority to find out what was happening, having called the airline herself only to be told things were too confused and panicked at the moment for any information to be given out by them. It was their way of saying they didn't know what was happening either!

But that didn't help her now, and after calling the hospital to check that both her mother and father were sleeping comfortably she rang the airport to book a flight out to England, only to be told the first available seat was late morning. She took it, knowing she was doing no good sitting here.

Dawn saw her seated at the breakfast bar in her galley-kitchen, drinking the remains of her third pot of coffee, the heavy look in her eyes evidence that she hadn't slept at all, her almost fixed gaze on the wall telephone telling its own story. Alex Hammond still hadn't called.

Her mother telephoned a short time later to assure her that her father was doing well, that he seemed a lot better. She seemed as perplexed as Morgan over Alex Hammond's silence.

Her suitcase was packed, her creased denims changed in favour of a tailored dress, her hair flowing freely about her shoulders, and she couldn't stand to sit here in her apartment another minute longer waiting for a call that obviously wasn't going to come, so she telephoned for a cab to take her to the airport.

When the doorbell rang a few minutes later she expected it to be the driver, but she opened the door to a barrage of questions and flashing intrusive lights.

'How do you feel about your sister's death, Morgan?'

'Will the funeral be here or in England?' asked another reporter.

'Will Glenna and her husband be buried together, Morgan?' persisted another.

Morgan had blanched at the sea of faces outside her apartment door; microphones and cameras were pushed into her face, a couple of them for television.

She had remained undisturbed by reporters all night, as her address was known to few but her closest friends, although it now seemed someone had released the wolves at her heels.

'Were you close to your sister, Morgan?' a beautiful, chic female asked at her continued numbed silence, and this avid curiosity about her grief sickened her.

'We hear your father collapsed when told of the crash—can you confirm this, Miss McKay?' one determined reporter pounced.

Morgan swallowed hard, unable to comprehend this hounding over such a private grief. What sort of people were they, to ask her such questions!

'Did you——'

'That will be enough!' rasped an authoritative voice, startling the members of the media into stunned silence.

A man was pushing his way through the crowd to Morgan's side, although he didn't need to push for long, for people stepped aside as they recognised a force stronger than themselves.

Alex Hammond. It could be no other man. She

might only have met him once, but the memory of him had stayed indelibly printed on her brain for some unknown reason. Possibly because she had never met anyone quite like him before.

Tall, taller even than Sam, he had a force of energy and determination that would make him stand out in any crowd; the dark hair was showing signs of greying at the temples now, the eyes were still the same icy grey she remembered, his nostrils flaring angrily now in his displeasure, his mouth thinned for the same reason. He wore a dark three-piece suit and snowy white shirt, and looked for all the world as if he hadn't just spent an exhausting eleven hours on a plane.

He grasped her arm in a vice-like grip. 'Let's go inside,' he muttered.

Morgan was only too pleased to comply, wondering why Alex Hammond had felt it necessary to fly over here rather than just telephone her. Unless he felt her father's collapse was enough on his conscience for one day! She could have told him she was past collapsing, that the long hours she had spent beside the telephone had at least given her time to calm, to realise that Glenna really was dead.

'Who the hell is he?' The members of the media weren't silenced for long. They might have recognised the authority of this man, but it was a recognition that had only made their curiosity all the deeper. 'Where did he come from?'

'With shoulders like that I don't care *where* he came from,' drawled the beautiful chic television reporter. 'I'm just glad he's here. Sir, are you a friend of Morgan McKay's?' There was more than a little personal interest in the blonde woman's question, although a microphone was thrust aggressively into Alex Hammond's face.

'I thought she was seeing Sam Walters,' murmured someone else.

Alex Hammond's hand had tightened on Morgan's arm at the intimacy of the woman reporter's words, and he pushed the microphone away from him with a dark scowl. 'I believe Miss McKay's privacy has been invaded enough for one day,' he snapped, his hand firm on her arm now as he turned her back into her apartment. 'If you'll excuse us—lady, gentlemen,' he nodded dismissively.

'Hey, the guy's English——'

'Your powers of deduction are amazing,' Alex Hammond taunted dryly, caring nothing for the ruddy hue that coloured the younger man's cheeks, pushing Morgan the rest of the way into her apartment and closing the door in the face of the renewed questioning. 'Like vultures!' he muttered as he followed her through to the lounge, then his silvery-grey eyes narrowed as he saw her packed suitcase standing next to a chair. He looked up at her with a frown. 'Are you going somewhere?'

'I—I'd given up on your call.' Her voice came out husky—and slightly defensive. She shouldn't need to explain herself to this man, damn it! 'I'm booked on a flight to England in a couple of hours' time.'

He merely nodded acknowledgement of the fact, seeming impatient to end the conversation before it had started. 'Is it true, has your father collapsed?'

Her antagonism faded as quickly as it had begun. Of course, her mother had said her father collapsed *after* Alex Hammond called—he didn't even know about it! 'It's true,' she admitted heavily. 'There's no danger, but it's hit him hard, harder than I realised. He wanted boys, you see,' she knew she was babbling, but she couldn't seem to control herself. 'That's why we were named Glenna and Morgan; he didn't have any names for girls.' She broke off. 'I'm sorry, you don't want to hear all this.' She avoided his all-seeing gaze, realising she had revealed too much of herself with these unguarded words.

She and Glenna had never doubted their father loved them, but they had always known of his desire for a son, had known their names had been chosen for boys and converted for the girls that had come in the place of the sons he wanted. She hadn't even realised her own feelings of inadequacy until she found herself telling it to Alex Hammond!

'I had no idea your father had collapsed.' He chose to ignore her lapse into the melancholy, confirming her thoughts that he hadn't known; his silver eyes were icy, his expression cold. 'Although it's been a shock to all of us.'

Then how did he manage to look so unmoved! Morgan knew she looked haunted, her parents and his mother were deeply shocked, and yet Alex Hammond looked—detached. There was no other way to describe the way he looked.

Morgan swallowed hard in the face of that detachment. 'They said—on the television—that there were no survivors.' She searched his face for some sign of that information being wrong. Not by the flicker of an eyelid did he show emotion. Oh, he was a cold bastard! She shuddered at the vehemence of her feelings, having taken even more of a dislike to this man.

'They were wrong,' he stated flatly.

Hope leapt in her heart. 'They were?'

'Yes. It appears—Sit down, please,' he told her abruptly.

She looked startled. 'I—I'm fine. I——'

'I said sit down, Morgan.' He didn't raise his voice, his expression didn't change, and yet Morgan sat, knowing the words were an order and not a request. 'It appears there were half a dozen survivors—all of them severely injured, but alive nonetheless.'

'Glenna——'

'Was not one of them. Neither was Mark.' Still the man showed no emotions.

Her breathing became ragged as the full impact of his words hit her. 'They—they're both dead?' she choked, having been given hope for a few seconds only to have it taken away from her again.

'Yes,' Alex Hammond stated flatly.

'Oh, *God*!' She hadn't realised how much hope she had still been harbouring, secretly believing that no news was good news. It was all gone now. She didn't doubt for a minute that Alex Hammond knew what he was talking about.

'But their son is very much alive,' his softly spoken words interrupted her weeping. 'And well.'

Morgan raised a tear-wet face, swallowing hard. 'Their—son?'

He nodded. 'Glenna was one of the survivors. She lived for two hours after the crash, badly—fatally injured herself. And somehow she kept alive long enough to give birth to her child. She had a son. His name—the name she chose for him—is Courtney.'

This time Morgan cared nothing for his lack of emotions. 'Courtney ...!' she gave a choked sound that was somewhere between a laugh and a cry. 'That's my father's name!'

'Yes,' Alex Hammond acknowledged. 'And I'm sure your father will be very proud of his grandson.'

'You—you've seen him?' She wiped away her tears with the back of her hand.

'Briefly,' he acknowledged tersely.

She was under control again now, hardly able to believe what he was telling her. Glenna had a son, a son who was alive! 'What does he look like? Is he like Glenna or Mark? Is——'

'He's like all newborn babies,' Alex Hammond dismissed impatiently. 'Small, pink, and he cries a lot. And incredibly like Glenna,' he added gruffly, showing he wasn't quite as unmoved by the baby's existence as he appeared.

'I want to see him,' she decided firmly.

'I have no doubt you will,' he drawled. 'But there's something else I think you should know before we go any further. Glenna also made provision for her son's future. She made you and me Courtney's legal guardians. Jointly,' he added pointedly.

CHAPTER TWO

MORGAN blinked; she was too stunned to do anything more than that. She was overjoyed, thrilled, at the thought of her nephew being alive and well. But she had no idea how both Alex Hammond and herself could be the baby's guardians, one living in England, the other in America.

Obviously Alex Hammond couldn't either. 'Of course it's impossible,' he said abruptly, placing his briefcase on her dining table. 'I have some documents here,' he unclicked the lock. 'Legal documents, drawn up by my lawyers, relieving you of all moral and legal obligation to Courtney.'

Morgan stood up slowly, feeling the anger burning up from within her. Just who did this man think he was! He came here and told her that her beloved sister was dead but that the child she had been expecting was alive. And now he calmly suggested she relinquish all rights to that child. The man was insane!

'No,' she told him bluntly.

He raised dark brows, halting in the removal of the official-looking papers from his briefcase. 'No?'

'Certainly not!' Her green eyes sparkled in challenge, her tall slender body as taut as a ripcord in her fury. 'Courtney is my nephew, and if my sister wanted me to be his guardian then that's what I intend being.'

'He has two guardians,' Alex reminded her. 'You *and* I.'

'So Glenna made a mistake,' Morgan snapped. 'Nobody's perfect!'

The haughty face took on an even more withdrawn

expression. 'I don't believe insults are going to help the delicacy of this situation,' he told her quietly.

'Neither is your insensitivity,' she glared at him. 'My sister has just died,' weakness washed over her in waves, 'and now you calmly suggest I reject her son from my life—my own nephew, my parents' only grandson!' Her voice rose shrilly.

'My nephew too, *my* mother's only grandson,' he pointed out dryly.

'But not her only grandchild! And when you have a son——'

'The same applies to you in regard to your own parents.'

She gave an impatient sigh at the way this man had an answer for everything. 'Giving up my guardianship of Court is not——'

'Courtney,' he substituted firmly.

'Court is short for——'

'He was named Courtney, let's stick to that, shall we?' he said abruptly.

'I'm sure Glenna meant it to be shortened to Court, like my father,' she insisted stubbornly.

'But Glenna isn't here——'

'You bastard!' Morgan choked raggedly. 'You cold-blooded, unfeeling bastard! You——' she sank slowly to the floor as blackness overcame her.

She woke up to find herself stretched full length on the corner unit sofa, her head propped up by several cushions, the darkly intent face of Alex Hammond bent over her. She snatched her hand away self-consciously as she realised it was held between long tapered fingers, the fingers of the other hand lightly tapping against her pale cheek.

Alex Hammond moved back instantly and sat back on his heels, seeming unexerted from having to carry her to the sofa; and she might be thin, but she wasn't a lightweight. Still, those shoulders and arms looked capable of great strength.

She sat up awkwardly, moving back and away from him. 'I'm sorry,' she said abruptly.

He nodded distantly. 'I've been expecting something like it ever since I arrived and found the press harassing you.'

'How clever of you!' Her voice was brittle.

Alex stood up, very dark and forbidding in Morgan's openly bright apartment, dwarfing it. 'You were at cracking point. I doubt you've slept all night. I had no idea of the added worry of your father's illness.'

Morgan swung her legs to the ground and stood up, feeling at less of a disadvantage, her own height being considerable, although Alex Hammond still topped her by a head. She swayed slightly as she stood, not as recovered as she thought she was, although her back was straight, her gaze steady as she faced Alex Hammond across the room. Like adversaries. And she had a feeling that was exactly what they were.

'It was waiting for your call that stopped me sleeping.' Her words were defensive because of the weakness she had shown by fainting in that way. 'You didn't have to come all the way to Los Angeles, you could have explained everything over the telephone and saved yourself the trouble of flying out here. I could have told you no just as easily that way,' she added hardly.

His mouth tightened. 'You won't even look at the papers I brought with me?'

'No.'

'Even though you know Courtney will be better off with us in England?'

'And who is *us*?' she derided scornfully. 'You and your mother? A bitter and resentful widow and an unfeeling man?'

Icy grey eyes raked over her with cool disdain. 'Or a fun-loving young actress with no morals?' he rasped.

'You mean *me*?' she gasped. 'Where did you get that impression, Mr Hammond?'

'Glenna was very proud of your first English televised role,' he drawled. 'We were all made to watch your undoubted talent as Mary-Beth Barker.'

That was what she had thought. 'Talent is the right word, Mr Hammond,' she taunted. 'I was acting a part—I thought you were intelligent enough to realise that.'

'Maybe I am,' he nodded. 'But I have no reason to believe Courtney would be happier with you than with us. You must work very hard, very long hours. I doubt you would have a lot of time to bring up a young child.'

She dismissed the wisdom of his words. Glenna had wanted her to have a part in bringing up Court, and that was what she was going to do. 'I have a plane to catch, Mr Hammond,' she told him briskly. 'I have to get to the airport.'

He closed his briefcase with a decisive click. 'I'll come with you.'

'That won't be necessary.'

'It's very necessary,' he told her grimly. 'I have a seat on that plane too.'

'Oh.' Her eyes were narrowed. 'You didn't intend staying long. Or were you so sure of what you thought my answer would be that you just expected to come here, have me sign those documents, and then return home?' Her eyes took on a dangerous sheen as she saw by the tightening of his mouth that that was exactly what he had thought. 'Glenna wasn't happy with your family, Mr Hammond,' she told him frostily. 'I'm beginning to understand why.'

'Indeed?' he bit out grimly.

'Yes!'

'And I'm beginning to see that you're as uncompromising as your sister was. Oh yes, we knew of Glenna's unhappiness,' he mocked her gasp of surprise. 'She made no secret of the fact. But I think I should point out once again that Glenna gave her son two guardians; she didn't cut the Hammonds out of Courtney's life as if she hated us.'

Morgan wondered if this man had a habit of always being right; if he did it was an annoying habit! 'Instead of arguing I suggest we get to the airport—I wouldn't want to miss the plane. I'll just go into my bedroom and call my mother at the hospital. She's been as anxious as I have.'

If Alex Hammond was affected by her deliberate move to shame him he didn't show it, settling his long length into a chair, sitting back to close his eyes with a weary sigh.

Guilt instantly washed over her. This man might seem like a cold robot to her, but his brother had just died, and he had just spent all those hours on a plane; he must be exhausted. 'Can I get you some coffee?' she offered huskily. 'Or something to eat?'

His eyes flickered open, silver-grey, showing no sign of the tiredness she suspected. 'Tea?' he queried hopefully.

Morgan smiled, and the tension instantly eased between them. 'I have tea,' she nodded. 'It's a habit I picked up when I went to England for the wedding. Milk, sugar?'

'Thanks,' he nodded.

Her mother came to the telephone straight away once she had been paged, and it was the hardest thing in the world to tell her that Glenna really was dead; her mother finally broke down now that she knew there was no hope of ever seeing her elder daughter again. Morgan broke down and cried with her, offering no resistance as Alex Hammond came in and took over, too overcome by grief herself now that her shock was passing to talk coherently.

'Your mother is overjoyed by her grandson's existence,' Alex Hammond rang off to assure her. 'She hopes she and your father can go to England to see him soon. In the meantime, I don't think you're in any condition to fly to England. Maybe it would be better——'

'I'm coming with you,' Morgan told him determinedly. 'I want to see Court-ney, and also I have to—to attend Glenna's funeral. Someone from the family should be there.' She went to the bathroom and washed her face in cold water. 'I take it the funeral will be in England.'

'As soon as—Yes,' he substituted abruptly. 'Eventually.'

Her spine stiffened at the addition of the last word. 'I understand,' she said heavily. 'I'm ready to leave now.'

'Are you sure——'

'I'm very sure.' Her expression was stubborn.

'Your work?'

'Will just have to wait,' she told him with bravado, not in the least sure how the studio would react to her taking off like this. They surely couldn't object to a couple of days, not in the circumstances. If they did they would just have to sue. She doubted they would want to do that. 'I intend coming with you, Mr Hammond—make no mistake about that.'

'Then perhaps you'd better call me Alex,' he derided. 'I don't intend calling you Miss McKay for the next twelve hours or so.'

'Morgan,' she supplied abruptly.

'I know that,' he nodded. 'Glenna spoke of you often.'

She would have liked to return the compliment, but Glenna had been surprisingly reticent about her brother-in-law, talking about him little, and then only in connection with Mark being at work. Apparently Alex Hammond kept to himself, spending little time with the family.

'Feel up to braving the media again?' he queried distantly. 'I doubt if they've left yet. Especially if news of survivors has filtered through.'

Completely in control of herself now, Morgan was able to move determinedly at Alex Hammond's side as they made their way downstairs to get into the cab that he had ordered to wait for them ten minutes ago as she cried. Alex ignored the questions thrown at them; his expression was distant, his hold on Morgan's arm unbreakable, despite the pushing and jostling going on about them.

'The airport,' he instructed the cab driver arrogantly, pushing Morgan in the car ahead of him.

She wasn't used to being dominated in this way. She had been brought up to be independent, to stand up for herself; Alex Hammond was obviously used to being dominant with the women in his life.

Morgan studied him curiously on the drive to the airport. There could be no doubting that he was very attractive, in an austere way, and yet Glenna had never mentioned him having a woman in his life. But he certainly didn't like men! His gaze had been critical of her, but it had definitely been male in its intent. No doubt there were women from time to time, just nothing serious. She wondered why. Alex was thirty-eight, surely that was quite old for a man not to have been married. He probably thought twenty-six was old for a woman not to have married either!

'Something funny?'

Her smile faded as she realised he was looking at her. 'Not really,' she dismissed. 'Is Courtney at your home?'

Alex shook his head. 'He's being kept in hospital for

a few days. It's a standard thing for new babies,' he added at her worried frown. 'He really is very well, Morgan. Perfectly healthy, even if he is eight weeks premature.'

'Thank God!' she shuddered.

'Yes,' he agreed curtly.

All was chaos at the airport; the members of the media who had been outside her home had obviously telephoned ahead to their colleagues, for a dozen or so reporters were continuing the harassment. Morgan wasn't in the least surprised when Alex secured a private lounge for them, and strode off to deal with their seats himself.

Morgan took this opportunity to call Sam and Jerry, something she hadn't had time to do in the trauma of the last hour. Sam was very understanding, and Jerry had already rearranged the work schedule to allow her to take a week off. A week should be long enough to convince the Hammonds that Glenna's baby belonged with her.

'Just don't be any longer than that,' Jerry warned in a growl, 'or the wrath of Zorbo will come down around your head!'

Morgan laughed softly, ringing off. Frank Zorbo was a small Greek man, the head of A.M.X. Broadcasting Company, and quite harmless until something put out his carefully organised programme schedule. Then he was like a roaring tornado.

'Everything is organised,' Alex came back to assure her. 'We'll be boarding in a few minutes.'

For the moment it just felt good to let him take over the details; her mind was not functioning as fluently as it usually did. Alex looked as if nothing ever deterred or upset him.

It came as a surprise to her when she was shown into the first class section of the plane, to the seat next to Alex Hammond. She had been booked into a seat much farther down the plane, had been told that there were no other seats available.

'I already had a seat reserved for you,' Alex told her at her qustioning look.

Her eyes widened. 'You *knew* I would be coming with you?'

'I told you, Glenna talked of you a lot. I was able to assess what your reaction would be.'

'But you flew over here yourself anyway?'

'It was worth a try,' he shrugged.

'Never,' she shook her head firmly. 'I'll never give Courtney up.'

Alex sighed. 'I suggest we save any further talk of the baby until a less emotional time.'

Morgan instantly felt guilty. This man had another long flight in front of him—he was likely to meet himself on the way back!—and what he needed at the moment was to rest. She deliberately stopped talking, although her tension began to rise as the engines of the plane roared for take-off. Everything had happened so suddenly, so quickly, that until this moment she hadn't given a thought to the flight itself. Glenna and Mark had just died in an aircraft very similar to this one, what if——

'It won't happen, Morgan.' Strong fingers clasped about hers, gently reassuring.

She had never thought of herself as a weak or dependent woman, and yet at that moment she was petrified, turning into the comfortable width of shoulder at her side, clinging on to Alex Hammond as if they were lovers.

Only when the plane was safely in the air did she move away from him. 'I'm sorry,' her lashes were downcast in her embarrassment at breaking down in that way. 'I'm not usually—well, I don't normally—'

'Forget it,' he dismissed abruptly. 'I already have.'

It wasn't the normal reaction a man had to holding her in his arms, and it irked her somewhat that this man was so immune to the female form. The man was a damned robot!

It didn't in the least surprise her when he fell asleep shortly after take-off, and she remained quietly at his side, guessing that he needed the rest. And if the truth were known she needed a little time to herself, to think quietly, to realise that she and the man at her side had sole responsibility for a tiny baby who would never know his real parents, who would be denied a mother's love. Morgan vowed on that long flight that she would be the mother to Courtney that Glenna had intended her to be—no matter what the Hammonds said or did!

Alex had left his Mercedes parked at the airport, and with the ease with which she was coming to expect from him he saw them through Customs and into the car, driving them to the Hammond house in Surrey himself.

'Courtney——'

'I'll drive you to see him tomorrow,' Alex interrupted abruptly. 'I believe we may be able to bring him home then.'

Morgan couldn't help the sudden rush of colour in her cheeks. It sounded curiously intimate for the two of them to be bringing home a baby. Obviously Alex thought so too.

'A nanny will be engaged for him,' he added harshly.

'No!'

'It's the best way——'

'It may be your best way, Alex,' she scorned, ignoring the tiredness still about his eyes, the fact that he must be feeling exhausted, knowing only that if she gave in to him over this then she would be continually doing so, 'but I happen to believe Courtney needs a mother's love, not the impersonality of a transient nanny.'

'A mother's love is something we can't give him!' Alex rasped.

'I can,' Morgan told him heatedly, her eyes flashing deeply green. 'I intend adopting him as my own son.'

Grey eyes snapped with anger. 'That might be a little difficult,' he ground out.

She eyed him warily. 'Why?'

'Both guardians have to agree to any plans involving Courtney,' he pointed out grimly.

She stiffened, turning in the leather seat to look at him, aware that he looked very weary, lines of strain beside his eyes and mouth, the latter a taut line of aggression. 'And you won't agree to my adopting Courtney?' she asked softly.

'No.'

'Why?'

'I don't believe it would be in his best interests.'

'Don't talk down to me, Alex Hammond!' she snapped. 'just say what you mean. You don't think a "fun-loving young actress with no morals" a suitable mother for him, that's it, isn't it?'

He sighed heavily. 'I wish I'd never made that remark. I suppose I'm to have it thrown up at me periodically during our association?'

'That won't be for long! I'm returning to Los Angeles as soon as possible.'

'Without Courtney.'

'*With* him.'

'No,' he shook his head. 'Not unless I agree. And I don't. Don't you think this is a little soon to start arguing about Courtney's future?'

'With you I have a feeling it's never too soon to start arguing!'

To her surprise the austere features broke into a

smile, and Alex instantly looked younger, incredibly
handsome, the grooves in his cheeks ones of humour
this time, unfamiliar grooves, as if he smiled little.
Morgan had a feeling that he didn't, and she wondered
at the reason for his harshness. A woman in the past,
perhaps? That was usually the reason a man with
Alex's intelligence retreated into himself. Perhaps he
hadn't been able to take rejection. Whatever the
reason, his humour now was totally unexpected. She
gave him a questioning look.

His mouth quirked. 'You're the only one who does
argue with me,' he drawled.

'Really?' She smiled too now.

'Really,' he nodded.

'That's incredible.'

'Yes.'

'And that's arrogant!'

'No,' he smiled again. 'It's quite exhilarating,
actually.'

Now why on earth should she blush like a schoolgirl
at the thought of Alex Hammond finding something
about her exhilarating? Maybe it was because he was a
challenge, the original ice man.

But she wasn't here to find him a challenge, she was
here to get Courtney and return home. And she *would*
do it.

It needed all her self-confidence to enter the
Hammond house with him a short time later; she was
wary about meeting Rita Hammond again. They
hadn't exactly taken to each other when they met two
years ago, and she had no reason to think the other
woman would be any more kindly disposed towards
her. The opposite if she also believed in the part of
Mary-Beth being Morgan's own nature!

If Rita Hammond had been sedated the day before
there was no sign of it today. The woman was tall,
almost as tall as her son, her iron-grey hair perfectly

coiffured, her make-up impeccable despite her sixty years, her taste in clothes sophisticated and flattering to her slender figure.

She looked at Morgan with flinty blue eyes, not surprised to see her, but not welcoming her either. Well, that suited Morgan, she wasn't glad to be here either!

'Miss McKay,' the other woman greeted regally.

'Mrs Hammond,' Morgan returned as frostily.

'You parents are well?'

Morgan's eyes widened. What was *wrong* with this family? This woman's son and daughter-in-law had been tragically killed and she was asking innocuous questions about Morgan's family! These people were emotionless. She need look no farther than Rita Hammond for her son's lack of emotion; these people obviously didn't know the meaning of the word love.

'Could I please go to my room?' she asked jerkily. 'I'm feeling—tired, after the journey.'

Rita Hammond instantly rang for Symonds, instructing him to take Morgan up to the 'lemon' room.

'We'll talk later,' Alex told her softly as she walked past him to follow Symonds upstairs.

She turned to smile at him, beginning to feel as if he was the only stability in a suddenly shaky world. 'You look tired,' she told him huskily. 'Why don't you rest too?'

Grey eyes widened—and then narrowed, almost as if he suspected her motives. 'Not yet,' he answered abruptly. 'I have things to do.'

'But soon, hmm?' she prompted.

'Perhaps,' he nodded distantly. 'Go with Symonds.'

She felt suitably dismissed, regretting the politeness of her concern. This man obviously didn't need anyone's sympathy for anything!

Morgan sat silently at Alex's side as they drove to the

hospital to pick up Courtney, so nervous her palms felt damp. It was ridiculous to feel so nervous about seeing a baby for the first time, but she couldn't help it. Babies were something she had no experience of, especially ones as young as Courtney. She didn't even know how to hold him—something Rita Hammond had taken great pains to point out to her.

Alex had obviously spoken to his mother by the time Morgan joined them for dinner the previous evening, for Rita Hammond was at her most haughty as she pointed out all the reasons Morgan wasn't equipped to take care of a baby. When Morgan had remained blandly adamant the older woman had resorted to insults. Even her son's curtly spoken words hadn't deterred her, until finally Alex suggested his mother retire to her room, where he accompanied her, returning only after his mother had fallen into a sedated sleep, apologising tersely for her rudeness, but making no excuses for it.

Morgan had slept fitfully, her body completely out of English time, and rose early, only to find Alex was up before her, having already breakfasted and doing some work in his study. Morgan had only just managed to contain her anxiety to leave and collect Courtney, waiting impatiently until Alex suggested it was time to go.

And now they were almost there. She was going to see Glenna's son at last!

He was beautiful! There was no other way to describe the tiny peaches and cream bundle wrapped in the white blanket. Tears filled her eyes as the nurse wheeled him out to them in his tiny crib, sleeping peacefully after his mid-morning feed.

'He's beautiful,' she breathed softly, her eyes wide with wonder 'Alex . . .!' She looked at him glowingly.

His expression softened. 'Why don't you dress him while I have a word with the doctor?'

She swallowed hard. She thought herself a pretty gutsy lady, but this tiny baby terrified her. 'I'll try.' She moistened her lips nervously, taking the box of expensive baby clothes that were part of a delivery made to the house early this morning. It seemed that the Hammond money could even get those sort of things delivered.

The nurse showed her into a private room, and between the two of them—with a lot of help from the nurse!—they managed to dress Courtney in the all-in-one blue suit. It still managed to swamp him despite being tiny. He was so incredibly like Glenna, with fiery-red hair and deep blue eyes, that Morgan felt fresh tears well up in her eyes.

'Go ahead and cry,' the nurse encouraged gently. 'It's always like this when a mother gets to take a premature baby home.'

Morgan blinked up at the young girl. 'Oh, but——'

'He's so much like you,' the nurse cooed at him gently. 'And I think he has your husband's jaw even now. He's going to be a strong-minded little boy.'

Morgan smiled at this young girl's misconception. Somehow the other girl had the impression that she and Alex were Courtney's parents. How angry he would be if he knew!

'I've been on holiday for a couple of weeks,' the girl unwittingly explained her mistake, 'so I missed Courtney's arrival into the world, but I can see he's done very well for a premature baby.' She helped Morgan put on the little woollen cap over Courtney's red curls. 'He has your colouring, you know,' she smiled.

'Probably a temper to go with it,' Morgan joined in the laughter, feeling a sense of elation at being in at the start of Courtney's life, seeing no reason to correct the young nurse's impression of her being his mother, not wanting the complications and sympathy such an explanation would evoke.

'Here's your husband now.' The girl moved to the door, smiling shyly up at Alex as he stood in the doorway.

Morgan looked at him, Courtney held firmly in her arms, wondering what his reaction was going to be to being thought her husband. The opinion he had of her morals, he would probably heatedly deny such a relationship.

'Ready, darling?' he asked huskily.

She nodded slowly, too stunned to answer him with words, and followed him out into the corridor.

'Good luck!' the young nurse beamed at them.

Alex gave her an abrupt nod, including a silver-haired woman in a blue uniform in that departing nod as they passed the office. 'Thank you—for everything,' he murmured softly to the woman.

Morgan allowed Alex to help her into the back of the dark Mercedes, still holding Courtney firmly in her arms, looking down in awe at his sleeping face. She looked up at Alex as he settled her more comfortably. 'Why——'

'Wait until we're on our way,' he rasped softly, closing the door with a soft click so that he didn't disturb the baby nestling against her.

Morgan had never experienced anything like the maternal love that flowed out of her for Courtney. It was a curiously choking feeling to know that he was totally dependent on her—on her *and* Alex. Alex had already made it clear that he intended taking a very strong part in Courtney's life, and she already knew him well enough to know he meant every word.

He spoke suddenly, interrupting her thoughts. 'As yet the media aren't aware of Courtney's existence,' he told her abruptly. 'I intend keeping it that way for as long as possible. That's why the deception at the hospital.'

'Deception?' she frowned.

'Courtney was registered as our child.'

'Ours?' she gasped.

He nodded. 'That's right.'

'You have a hell of a nerve——'

'Ssh, you'll wake the baby,' he mocked her anger. 'And I'm sure you have no idea what to do if that happens.' He eyed her mockingly in the driving mirror. 'No comeback?'

'None,' she shrugged. 'But I bet you don't know either,' she said with satisfaction.

'Wrong,' he returned smugly.

Her eyes widened. 'Wrong?'

He nodded. 'I have it all written down. Compliments of the Ward Sister.'

'That's cheating!'

'Common sense,' he corrected. 'I even have a bottle in case he wants feeding.'

'Too clever by half,' she mumbled, feeling too elated from holding Courtney in her arms to feel any real anger with Alex. Holding the tiny baby gave her a sense of well-being, as if she held a tiny part of Glenna to her.

Glenna would have loved Courtney, she had been looking forward to his birth so much. No wonder she had clung to life long enough to give birth to him. If only her strange decision to make Alex Hammond and herself Courtney's guardians could be explained that easily!

Although Alex seemed more approachable today, less inclined to be the austere stranger she was used to. Perhaps Courtney's innocence had got to him too. Although she wouldn't count on it! No doubt he would revert to type soon enough.

'Damn, damn, *damn!*' he muttered as they entered the long driveway to the house, and slowed the car down.

'What is it?' Morgan sat forward concernedly,

Courtney still—thank goodness!—fast asleep in her arms.

'I hope you feel up to facing the press again,' he ground out. 'Why the hell didn't my mother ring the police and have them thrown off my land!' he bit out grimly as he halted the car and was instantly surrounded by obvious members of the press, tape-recorders and cameras at the ready. 'There's going to be no keeping Courtney's existence a secret now,' he turned to mutter. 'Just stay at my side, Morgan, and don't say a word!'

What did he take her for! He treated her as if she was some sort of brainless idiot, not a woman of twenty-six. Who did——

'And calm down,' he taunted at the flash in her green eyes. 'You don't want them to think you hate me, do you?' he mocked before swinging out of the car to walk round and open the door for her, ignoring the questions being thrown at him as if he didn't hear them.

'Is this your nephew, Mr Hammond?' The jostling became more intense as Morgan stepped out of the car with Courtney in her arms.

'The son of Glenna McKay and your brother Mark?' they persisted as Alex guided her towards the house.

'Is this Morgan McKay, sir?' another tried politeness.

'Of course it is,' another man said eagerly. 'Don't you watch her in *Power Trap?*' His tone implied appreciation of the character she played. 'It's been rumoured that you and Miss McKay are the baby's guardians,' the man followed them as they walked up the steps to the house. 'Do you have any comment to make about that, Mr Hammond?'

Again Alex ignored the question, although Morgan could see by the tightening of his mouth that he was angry such information had become public knowledge.

'Does this mean that, in the best tradition of romances, the two of you will be marrying?' the man persisted.

Morgan knew she had blanched, and she could see that Alex had stiffened at such a suggestion. She and Alex marry? Never!

CHAPTER THREE

HER arm felt bruised from the way Alex thrust her inside the house, closing the door in the young man's face as he continued his questioning.

Morgan had never been so shocked in her life. Where did people get these ideas from? She and Alex hardly knew each other, and what they did know they disliked. They would certainly never consider *marrying* each other, not even for Courtney's sake.

Alex was scowling heavily as his mother came out of the lounge, throwing his car keys down carelessly on the hall table. 'Have you called the police, Mother?' he rasped.

'Police?' Rita Hammond looked puzzled. 'Oh, you mean the press,' she dismissed.

'Of course I mean——'

'Alex, you had no right to take that woman with you to collect *my* grandson!' Her icy blue eyes spat venom at Morgan.

He frowned. 'Are you saying *you* told the media?' he asked softly.

'No, of course not,' the elderly woman snapped, striding over to stand in front of Morgan. 'Give him to me,' she ordered, holding out her arms for the baby.

Morgan's arms tightened about the tiny shawl-wrapped form. She didn't like the almost hysterical gleam in Rita Hammond's eyes. She had been wrong about this woman's lack of emotion concerning Glenna and Mark's death; Rita Hammond was slowly cracking up, her emotions held on too tight a rein.

Morgan looked appealingly at Alex, and was

relieved when he stepped forward to take control of the situation.

'It's time for your medication, Mother——'

'I don't want it,' his mother refused imperiously, shaking off his hand on her arm. 'It just makes me sleepy. If I hadn't been sleeping this morning I could have come with you to collect Courtney. *She* has no right to him!'

'Mother——'

'She's a slut, Alex, just like her sister was. I will not permit her into my grandson's life!' Rita Hammond's voice was beginning to rise shrilly. 'You should know that no member of that family is capable of bringing up a child decently!' Her eyes glittered with hatred.

Morgan was very pale. 'Mrs Hammond——'

'Give the baby to me!' The other woman reached out for Courtney, and Morgan stepped back out of her reach. There was no way she was going to relinquish the baby to this hysterical woman!

'Mother——'

'Give him to me!' Rita Hammond began pulling at her arms, waking the baby, who instantly gave a heartrending wail of hunger. 'You see?' she turned triumphantly to her son. 'Courtney doesn't like her either. He's frightened of her. Alex, I forbid this woman to come near my grandson.'

'Let's go to your room, Mother,' Alex controlled her, firmly propelling her out of the room, not sparing a second glance for the shocked and pale Morgan.

What did Rita Hammond mean by calling Glenna a slut? How dared she talk about Glenna like that, and imply that she was the same! The woman might be bordering on collapse, but her insults to Glenna were unforgivable.

'Shall I take the baby for his feed, Miss McKay?'

She turned at the softly spoken words, her eyes widening as she took in the neat nurse's uniform and kindly face of the middle-aged woman standing in front of her, her arms held out for Courtney.

'I believe he's hungry, Miss McKay,' the woman added pointedly as the baby continued to scream.

Anger warred with practicality, and finally it was the latter that won. Courtney was hungry, extremely so by the sound of him, and as she had no idea what Alex had done with his bottle Morgan had no choice but to hand the baby over to the capable-looking woman.

'Mr Hammond engaged you?' she asked casually as the woman held Courtney confidently in her arms.

'Of course,' the woman nodded. 'I've prepared the nursery in your absence. If you'll excuse me . . .'

Morgan nodded abruptly; Courtney's lungs sounded as if he were going to burst if someone didn't feed him soon! But Alex's decision to engage a nurse for him without even consulting her was unforgivable, especially when she had already made her feelings about such an idea clear.

He hadn't returned from his mother's room after ten minutes' wait, and with an angry sigh Morgan went up to her room to shower and change for lunch. What she had to say to him couldn't wait much longer. Glenna might have been treated like an outcast in this family—Rita Hammond's words more than showed that!—but *Morgan* McKay wasn't tied by love to any member of this family, and she wouldn't let them walk all over her.

She lunched alone, although the absence of the reporters in the driveway told her that Alex had been in touch with the police. A casual query to Symonds as to Alex's whereabouts now told her he was in his study. That was all she needed to know!

Alex told her to come in after her firm knock on the door, and she stood aggressively in front of his desk, refusing his offer to sit down. She didn't intend feeling at a disadvantage by sitting across from him like some naughty schoolgirl!

'You engaged a nanny——'

'Nurse,' he corrected calmly. 'Courtney is with her now?' He raised dark brows enquiringly.

She nodded abruptly. 'He's been fed, and is now fast asleep in his crib. I checked on him before lunch,' she explained.

'I believe Mrs Ford is very capable,' he nodded.

'And I believe I told you I didn't want Courtney to have a nanny——'

'Mrs Ford is a nurse,' he repeated, sitting back, his eyes narrowed as if for battle.

'Nanny, nurse, it's all the same!' she said heatedly.

Cool grey eyes raked over her disdainfully. 'Courtney is a premature baby, he was born in unusual circumstances. The doctors only agreed to him coming home with us today on the understanding that an experienced nurse be engaged to monitor his progress for a few weeks.'

'Oh.'

'Indeed,' he drawled at her discomfort.

Angry colour flared in her cheeks. 'You could have told me that, damn you! You didn't say a damned word on the drive to the hospital, or on the way back.'

'I had other things on my mind——'

'Your hysterical mother for one, I hope,' she snapped.

'Let's leave my mother out of this,' he bit out harshly.

'Let's not,' Morgan shot back at him tautly. 'She threw out some insults before lunch that need explaining.'

Alex put down his pen, standing up restlessly. 'Why do you persist in pursuing subjects that would be better left for the moment?' he bit out, his eyes narrowing angrily.

'And why do you persist in avoiding them?' she snapped, as tense as he was, and not just because of the things his mother had said about Glenna. She still hadn't got over the shock of the suggestion that she and this man should marry for Courtney's sake. It would have been laughable, if the reporter hadn't been so damned serious. 'So far you've opted out of discussing Courtney's furture, and now you won't tell me the reason for your mother's hatred of Glenna.'

A nerve pulsed erratically in his hard cheek. 'Did it ever occur to you that I am as deeply affected at this doubled loss as you and my mother appear to be?' he rasped. 'Did you ever think I might have some grief of my own to contend with?' His mouth twisted as contrition washed over her. 'I can see you didn't,' he said abruptly. 'And maybe I don't show my emotions as easily as you do, but that doesn't mean I don't have them. Mark was my young brother, and Glenna had been a member of my family for two years. Maybe I haven't been showing my feelings before now, but you and my mother have been displaying enough hysteria for all of us!' he scorned hardly.

She swallowed hard, feeling the chastisement for what it was. Just because the man gave the impression of being of stone it didn't mean he was without feelings. 'I'm sorry,' she said stiltedly. 'We'll— postpone this discussion then.'

His mouth twisted with dry humour. 'Only postpone it?'

'Your mother's words against Glenna were pretty insulting.'

'She's at breaking point, surely you can see that?' Alex dismissed.

She nodded. 'But it's usually when we're under the most emotional strain that we can dare to say the things we really feel.'

'My mother is always—articulate,' he drawled

derisively. 'Believe me, she always says what she feels.'

'Like you.'

'And you,' he nodded.

Unwilling humour lightened her features. 'Pretty honest lot, aren't we?' she mocked.

'I would say so,' Alex agreed wryly. 'Now would you mind if I got on with my work? Hammond Industries, unfortunately, hasn't ground to a halt, I still have to run it.'

He was kept very busy the next three days, so much so that Morgan rarely saw him. She didn't see too much of Rita Hammond either, as Alex had persuaded the other woman to stay with her daughter for a while. Her absence was a welcome relief to Morgan. She spent almost every waking moment with Courtney, and soon lost her nervousness with him, managing to feed, dress and change him with ease now. And the baby seemed to be coming to know her too, often stopping his crying if she should happen to take him in her arms and cradle him, when he wouldn't stop for Mrs Ford.

Morgan came to a halt in the nursery doorway on the third evening when she saw Alex actually sitting in the rocker in the nursery feeding Courtney his evening bottle. As far as she was aware he had never done such a thing before.

As if becoming aware of her gaze on him he looked up, giving a rueful grimace at her surprised expression.

'You're doing very well,' she smiled, moving further into the room.

'I thought I was,' he nodded. 'Until I winded him and he was sick down my back!'

Morgan held back her laugh with difficulty. 'I had a few accidents like that to start with, but now I always put a towel over my shoulder.'

'I will in future.' He put the bottle down as it was finished with.

'Here, let me,' she draped a towel over his shoulder.

'A bit late for that, isn't it?' he mocked.

'Better late than never,' she quipped, wiping Courtney's mouth as he was a little sick. 'See,' she said with satisfaction. 'He's almost asleep,' she murmured softly a few minutes later, as the baby's head turned to one side and his eyes closed.

Alex stood up to lay the drowsy baby gently back in his crib. 'I sent Mrs Ford to dinner and thought I would see what it was that's given you that glow for the last few days.'

'Well, it wasn't having Courtney being sick down my back,' she retorted to hide her embarrassment. She hadn't been aware of having a glow, or the fact that Alex had noticed it.

He eased the dampness of the silk material from his shoulders. 'God, my shirt stinks!'

'So will you,' she assured him. 'I should get that shirt washed immediately. And you'll need a shower.'

'And I always thought babies smelt of talcum powder!'

'Poor Alex!' she laughed softly.

'Hm,' he grimaced. 'I didn't deprive you of your nightly treat, did I? Mrs Ford tells me you've been mainly feeding and caring for Courtney yourself.'

'I've enjoyed it.' It also gave her something to do. She was left mainly to her own devices, Alex either at work or in his study, and she liked being with Courtney.

He nodded, moving out of the nursery and into the corridor so that their conversation didn't disturb the sleeping baby. 'The funerals are tomorrow, Morgan,' he told her quietly. 'They've been arranged for the afternoon.'

She had paled at his first mention of funerals. She

had known that the bodies from the crash had been released for burial now, but Alex hadn't mentioned the funerals to her before.

'I've spoken to your parents,' he continued in the emotionless voice that she so hated. 'Your father still isn't well enough to travel, and your mother doesn't feel she should leave him at such a time.'

'Of course not,' she snapped. She knew exactly how her father was; she had telephoned America several times since her arrival here. The closeness she had felt to Alex while they were with Courtney had completely gone, and the resentment was now back with a vengeance. 'You should have let me tell them.'

'It wasn't necessary——'

'They're my parents, damn it!'

'Why do you always resort to swearing when you lose your temper?' he bit out.

'Why do you always *make* me lose my temper?' she flashed.

'I have no idea,' he said grimly.

'I do!' she glared at him, her eyes sparkling deeply green. 'You have to be the most arrogant, bossy individual I've ever had the misfortune to meet. You had no right to talk to my parents about the funerals— I should have done it!'

'I didn't want to cause you any more pain——'

'You mean you were too busy organising everyone to consider anyone else's feelings but your own,' she dismissed scathingly. 'I've been in control of my own life since I left home at eighteen to go to college, and then you come along, with your dictatorial ways and expect everyone to jump on command. Well, I *don't* jump, Mr Hammond, and quite frankly I never will!'

He listened to her tirade in stony silence, a man who ran and owned an empire, who made decisions every day that affected thousands of lives, and the fact that one mere woman, one *unwelcome* woman in his home, dared to question his authority obviously came as a great and unexpected shock to him.

'I intend returning to the States after—after the funerals,' she told him coldly. 'But only for a couple of weeks at most. And then I'll be back. And I'll fight for custody of Courtney with every weapon I can think of.'

Alex shook his head. 'I can't let you have him.'

'Because you consider my morals aren't good enough?' she taunted. 'You'll find nothing wrong with them, no matter how deeply you dig into my past. I've been too busy with my career the last few years to want to complicate my life with emotional entanglement, especially with Glenna's marriage as an example! She loved your brother, and yet she was still unhappy. I didn't want that for myself.'

'Glenna mentioned someone called Sam.' He looked at her with narrowed eyes.

She flushed. 'It would seem you spent a considerable amount of time talking to my sister.'

He nodded distantly. 'She was an intelligent woman, and Mark wasn't always here. Glenna naturally told me about you, your parents—Sam.'

'I've been seeing him for several months. But I certainly don't intend marrying him.'

'I trust he knows that?'

'None of your business, Mr Hammond,' she snapped.

'No,' he sighed, 'I don't suppose it is. All right, Morgan, have your time back in the States. But when you get back here don't expect to take Courtney away from me. He's a Hammond, he'll stay here where he belongs.'

'We'll see about that!'

'Indeed we will,' he drawled confidently, and left her to go to his bedroom to change his shirt.

It was his confidence that worried her the most. He

was almost *too* confident, as if she didn't have a chance of getting Courtney. And maybe she didn't. She had a lot against her—her job, her single state, the fact that Courtney had been born a British citizen. But she wouldn't give up without a fight, wouldn't be her father's daughter if she did that!

Morgan decided she hated funerals. She had never been to one before, had never had reason to, and those two coffins standing side by side in the church, all that remained of Glenna and Mark, seemed all the more heartrending.

Alex stood at her side, had supported his mother all through the service as she seemed about to collapse. Morgan had driven to the church with them, Janet and Charles Fairchild travelling in the car behind them, their two little girls being left with Charles' mother for the day.

Morgan hated being in this cold emotionless church, hated the curious looks Mark's family directed at her, and she wondered why she didn't cry when it was her sister lying in one of those boxes.

She refused to cry, refused to believe that any part of Glenna, the laughing beautiful woman that mattered, was anywhere near this sterile service, this stark church. None of these people here had loved Glenna, none had tried to understand her—and her sister wouldn't give them the satisfaction of knowing how deeply she mourned her.

By the time they got back to the house Rita Hammond seemed to have recovered her composure, and was acting the gracious hostess as the family began to arrive from the church.

To Morgan it was just another part of the charade. How could these people genuinely feel the loss of two beautiful young people when they could stand around drinking sherry and eating the trays of food the staff were circulating with? Morgan couldn't have eaten a thing and, quite frankly, the whole thing made her feel sick.

She wanted to escape, to get away from here, and yet pride kept her standing in the room, that and her love for Glenna. Her sister hadn't been one to run away from a fight, and neither would she.

'She finally got her wish.'

Morgan spun round to confront Janet Fairchild, instantly tensing. Janet was as cold and calculating as her mother. She even looked like her with her cold blue eyes and tightly drawn back black hair, and Morgan knew any attempt at conversation with her owed nothing to politeness.

'I beg your pardon?' she said warily.

'Glenna,' Janet drawled, dressed completely in black as was her mother; Morgan had chosen a less dramatic navy blue dress, not being out to make any impressions. 'She always wanted to get away from the family,' she taunted. 'She got her wish—although hardly in the way she expected.'

Morgan drew in a harsh breath of pain. 'That's a disgusting thing to say!'

Janet raised dark brows, coolly knocking the ash from her cigarette into the ashtray. 'Is it? Perhaps. But it's the truth, isn't it?' she shrugged.

'Glenna was unhappy here, yes. But——'

'You knew about that?'

She frowned. 'I don't think Glenna ever made any secret of the fact that she was—dissatisfied, with her life here.'

'She wanted her career,' Janet scorned. 'Mark should never have married an actress. It was obvious a woman like that could only be interested in his money.'

Morgan gasped. Janet was more like her mother than she had previously realised, both of them seeming to take delight in insulting the dead Glenna. 'Must I remind you that Glenna is—was—my sister?' her voice shook a little, and she saw the other woman's mouth twist derisively at this show of weakness.

Janet gave a dismissive snort. 'You don't need to remind me of anything; you're like Glenna in a lot of ways.'

This time the insult was a personal attack, and Morgan didn't hesitate to retaliate. 'Did she also think you were a vicious bitch?' she asked coolly.

Angry colour flooded the other woman's cheeks. 'Glenna had more sense than to be openly hostile,' she snapped.

She raised her brows, the brightness of her hair secured at her nape. 'And I don't?' she drawled. 'I'm sorry, Mrs Fairchild, I thought this was honesty time.'

'It is.' Blue eyes flashed their dislike. 'I don't like you any more than I did Glenna. We'll certainly never make the mistake of letting another McKay into the family!'

'Courtney is half McKay.'

'I meant you, Morgan.' Janet looked at her with dislike. 'I'm telling you this in case you got the wrong idea from the newspapers.'

'That I marry Alex!' she gasped.

'Exactly.'

'Wouldn't he have some say as to who he married?' she derided.

'Of course,' Janet snapped her impatience. 'And I can tell you now that he doesn't intend marrying anyone.'

Morgan gave a bored shrug. 'You're safe then, aren't you?'

'Unless you try to force the issue,' the other woman studied her with narrowed eyes, 'Alex will allow no harm to come to Courtney.'

'I would never harm him!' she bit out angrily, tiring

of this conversation with this vindictive woman. 'Must I remind you that this is a funeral, Mrs Fairchild? Hardly the place for the things you're saying!'

'I can think of no better place,' Janet rasped. 'Glenna has created trouble, as always,' she snapped. 'She must have known the havoc this joint guardian-ship would cause.'

'She was hardly in any condition to think of hitting back at the Hammonds at the time,' Morgan told the other woman tautly.

'Your sister was an embarrassment to my family from the day she came into it!'

Her mouth twisted. 'Didn't she come up to your strict family standards?'

'No!' Janet snapped. 'And she never would have done. If she hadn't become conveniently pregnant I doubt if the marriage would have lasted as long as it did.'

'Conveniently . . .?' Morgan echoed sharply. 'Are you implying that Glenna became pregnant on purpose?'

'Exactly. Providing the Hammond heir was guaran-teed to keep her the wife of a wealthy man. Except that I know for a fact that Mark didn't want children yet.'

Morgan shrugged. 'Accidents happen.'

'Not to Mark,' Janet told her pointedly.

Morgan paled, swallowing convulsively. 'Are you saying—Are you implying——'

'That someone else was involved in Courtney's conception?' the other woman drawled. 'Someone other than Mark? I'm saying it's a distinct possibility,' she shrugged.

'I don't believe it!' Morgan said heatedly. 'You're just saying these things. Glenna would never have an affair. She loved Mark very much.'

'And she knew her marriage was failing. She

wouldn't be the first woman to deliberately have a child in order to keep her marriage together—even another man's child.'

'I don't believe that,' Morgan repeated coldly. 'Glenna wasn't capable of what you're accusing her of.'

Janet's mouth twisted derisively. 'Believe me, she was,' she taunted.

Morgan was breathing deeply, so angry she wanted to actually hit this woman. The character of Mary-Beth would know how to handle this situation with a confidence that would strip this woman of all her arrogance. Unfortunately she didn't have an ounce of Mary-Beth in her! 'Are you really serious about Courtney not being Mark's child?' she frowned.

'Very serious,' the other woman nodded. 'But my mother believes he's Mark's son, and that's all that matters.'

'A blood test——'

'Might prove my point,' Janet acknowledged tauntingly. 'And then again it might not. But could you do that to your own sister, your *dead* sister?'

Morgan paled, knowing that Janet Fairchild was right. Even supposing Glenna had done such a thing— which she seriously doubted!—she couldn't do anything to hurt her sister's memory. Her parents would never forgive her if she did that. Besides, she didn't believe for one moment that Glenna had been involved with another man; despite her unhappiness in England Glenna had continued to love her husband.

'I thought not,' the other woman derided. 'Go back to America, Morgan. You aren't wanted here.' She strolled off, smiling at several of the other guests as she went, just as if she hadn't just dealt Morgan a wounding blow.

Morgan looked up as she sensed someone watching her, and her eyes clashed with questioning grey ones. Alex stood across the room talking to an elderly man, but his attention was only half held by the conversation, the rest of it concentrated on her. She turned away from that probing glance, needing to escape, needing to be alone to think of all that Janet Fairchild had so enjoyed telling her.

She moved to the doorway, glancing round, suddenly aware that Alex was making his way towards her. She didn't want to talk to him now, and she breathed a sigh of relief as one of the numerous relatives waylaid him, slipping out of the room unnoticed by any but those all-seeing grey eyes.

Mrs Ford was in the nursery with Courtney, cuddling the unusually fretful baby. 'I think he ate too much,' she smiled as Morgan came into the room.

'Probably,' she smiled, knowing her nephew's appetite well. 'Would you like to go down to the kitchen and get yourself a cup of tea?' she offered. 'I'll stay with Courtney.'

'Well, if you're sure . . .?'

'Very,' she nodded, knowing that after Janet Fairchild's vehemence Courtney's innocence was what she needed.

'Thank you,' Mrs Ford smiled. 'I won't say it wouldn't be very welcome.'

Morgan took the crying Courtney from the other woman, her expression softening as she gazed down at his cherubic features; he had filled out in just the last week. He stopped crying as soon as she took him into her arms.

'He knows.' The nurse looked down at them, her own expression softened by the lovely picture Morgan made holding the baby.

Morgan was bemused by the perfection of the tiny human being in her arms; she never ceased to be amazed by how beautiful her nephew was. 'Knows?' she echoed softly, deep blue eyes staring up at her as Courtney sucked on his fist.

'That you love him,' Mrs Ford murmured. 'Oh, I love him too, but he senses that it isn't the same as what you feel for him. Babies are very intelligent when it comes to the people who care for them.'

She wondered if that were the reason Courtney invariably cried when Rita Hammond or her daughter picked him up. And why he slept in Alex Hammond's arms? Alex was a part of this hateful family too, and yet Courtney instinctively trusted him.

'I shouldn't be long,' the nurse nodded.

Morgan didn't mind how long she was, she had no inclination to go back downstairs and join the vultures, would much prefer to spend the time with Courtney.

But she couldn't stop herself from looking for some resemblance to Mark in the sleepy features beneath her. The bright red hair was strictly Glenna, the blue eyes, normal in most newborn babies, could have come from either parent. Of course there was the determination in the little chin that the nurse at the hospital had noticed, but Glenna had been very forceful, and Morgan had a stubborn streak herself. No, there was not one feature to distinguish Courtney as a Hammond.

'I thought I might find you here.'

She looked up at the sound of that familiar raspy voice, looking straight into Alex Hammond's harsh face. He leant against the door-jamb watching her. She wondered how long he had been standing there; she hadn't been aware of his presence until he spoke.

Colour flushed her cheeks as she recalled her thoughts of a few minutes ago. Did this man also think Glenna had had an affair, that Courtney wasn't his brother's child? He gave no indication of harbouring any such thoughts about Glenna, but then he wasn't a man who gave away much of his thoughts, about anything. And perhaps if it were the truth his mother's resentment towards Glenna needed no further explanation.

'I couldn't stand that circus any longer,' she told him coldly, at once on the defensive.

His mouth tightened, but he gave no other indication of his anger, and his voice was mild when he spoke. 'Would you rather no one had shown their respect?'

'Respect I could understand. That,' she nodded in the direction of downstairs, 'is no better than a farce. They act as if this was a party!'

'Would you rather they all stood about crying?'

'At least it would be more natural!'

He gave an impatient sigh. 'You call hiding in here natural?' he scorned. 'You can put Courtney down now,' he derided. 'He's been asleep for several minutes.'

She glanced down at the sleeping baby, then stood up to place him in his crib, putting her hands awkwardly together now that she had nothing else to occupy them. She faced Alex uncomfortably across the room.

'Why is it we always meet in the nursery?' he asked softly.

Morgan moistened her lips. 'I—I spend a lot of my time in here.'

'I wasn't criticising,' he said gently. 'Merely stating a fact.'

'The facts are, Mr Hammond, that the funerals are no more than a valid excuse for your mother to act the gracious hostess,' all her resentment came to the fore to be directed at this man, 'and that I have just been highly insulted by your sister.'

'Janet?' he frowned.

'Do you have another one?' she derided.

'What did she say to you?' His eyes were narrowed to grey slits.

'It isn't important that you know her exact words,' she shrugged dismissively; the enormity of what Janet Fairchild had said to her was still too new to take in—

or share with this man. 'Some of it wasn't unlike the remarks you made to me when you came over to Los Angeles,' her head went back in challenge.

His mouth tightened ominously. 'I thought we'd agreed that I regret that remark.'

'*You* agreed,' she said aggressively. 'I said nothing.'

'Morgan——'

'Yes?' She met his gaze defiantly.

A pulse beat erratically in his dark cheek. 'I'm trying hard to understand that your behaviour is because of the pain and loss you must be feeling today, but don't push me too far,' he warned softly.

'Don't push *you* too far?' she repeated incredulously, angrily. 'I'm supposed to take any sort of insult this family dishes out, and you say *I'm* pushing *you* too far! Well, I have news for you—Oh!' she gasped as she was pulled roughly against the hardness of his body. 'Alex?' Her eyes were wide with apprehension at the fierceness of his expression.

'Yes—Alex,' he ground out, his eyes darkening almost to black as he looked down at her with savage intensity. 'God, Morgan, you're so beautiful!' he frowned, his head lowering as his lips claimed hers.

It was the last thing she had expected from this man, and her mouth parted in a gasp of surprise as his lips met hers, allowing him to deepen the kiss, to go further, deeper, into the moist recesses.

She had melted at his first touch, felt pleasure at the intimacy of his kiss as he continued the slow druging movement, curving her body into the hardness of his, his hands moving restlessly from her thigh to her breasts.

The kiss might have gone on for ever, might have become more than a kiss, both of them caught up in the breathless moment of passion. But the sound of a gasp from the open doorway had them pulling apart, to see Rita Hammond looking at them in horror.

CHAPTER FOUR

MORGAN was the first to move, pulling out of Alex's arms. For a moment they tightened about her, then he released her, turning to look at the woman in the doorway with steely eyes.

'Did you want something, Mother?' he asked coldly.

Morgan had to admire his cool. Frankly, she was a little disconcerted herself. The kiss from Alex Hammond had been totally unexpected, her reaction volcanic. In fact, she couldn't ever remember responding to anyone as she had responded to Alex. Rita Hammond's interruption had been achingly unwelcome. Her mouth still throbbed from Alex's possession, her senses still aroused.

His mother drew herself up to her full impressive height. 'I came to tell you Uncle Simon is leaving. I had no idea I would be interrupting—something,' she looked at Morgan with haughty disdain, as if it were all her fault that she had walked in and found her son kissing her.

Alex strode over to the door. 'Shall we go downstairs, Mother?' he prompted hardly, giving no answer to her pointed reference to him kissing Morgan.

'I'd like to talk to Morgan——'

'It can wait,' he bit out abruptly.

'But——'

'I'll talk to you later, Morgan.' Alex turned to her, cutting off his mother's protest. 'All right?' His voice had gentled.

'Er—yes,' she swallowed hard. 'Okay.'

Alex took his mother with him, his hand firm on her

elbow. Morgan was relieved at his thoughtfulness; the last thing she needed was a run-in with Rita Hammond. Besides, she needed to assimilate her own feelings.

Alex Hammond had always seemed so distant, so remote, she couldn't believe he had kissed her with such passion. And she had kissed him back. It hadn't been an ordinary kiss either; his mouth on hers had affected her like no other. She was adult enough to realise that something momentous had happened to her when Alex kissed her. She was also adult enough to realise she didn't welcome the complication of being sexually attracted to him. How could she even attempt to fight him over Courtney when he affected her this way, when he would only have to touch her for her to melt in his arms and give him anything he asked for—including herself! It was unbelievable, incredible, and yet she knew it was true.

The guests were starting to leave when she at last went downstairs, and she saw with some relief that Janet and her husband had already left. Although Rita Hammond eyed her with dislike, and Morgan couldn't quite meet that accusing gaze, feeling almost guilty. Which was ridiculous. Alex had initiated that kiss—she had merely responded! And she would again if he should ever want to kiss her again; she knew that even though they argued constantly that Alex was the first man ever to elicit that unreserved response from her.

Rita Hammond watched the two of them closely during dinner, almost as if she expected them to be unable to keep their hands off each other. Morgan held back her amusement with effort, although Alex looked angry by his mother's behaviour.

'Will you come to my study for a while?' he requested huskily of Morgan after the meal. 'I'd like to talk to you before you leave tomorrow.'

Her pulse began beating faster at the thought of

being alone with him again, and she wondered if he would kiss her.

'Surely whatever you have to say to Morgan can be said in front of me, Alex?' his mother put in curtly.

'No,' he pulled back Morgan's chair for her as she stood up, 'I don't think it can.'

The older woman flushed. 'Why not?'

He viewed her arrogantly. 'If I were to tell you that I wouldn't need to talk to Morgan alone.'

'Then——'

'If you'll excuse us?' Alex said tautly.

'But, Alex——'

'Later, Mother,' he dismissed hardly, manoeuvring Morgan out of the room with his hand firm on her elbow.

Morgan studied him beneath lowered lashes. He certainly was forceful! When he said no one argued with him, he really meant no one. Rita Hammond had looked furious!

And Alex looked magnificent, his black dinner suit fitting him superbly, emphasising the lean strength of his body, the white silk shirt making his skin appear darker. Morgan wondered why she hadn't been aware of his attractiveness earlier.

A small fire had been lit in the study, the evenings beginning to cool to autumn now. Morgan moved to the chair opposite his across the desk, unconsciously graceful in the clinging black dress, her arms and throat bare, the dress caught over one shoulder in a Grecian style.

'Come and sit over here,' Alex invited huskily, standing next to the leather sofa in front of the fire. 'It's more comfortable.'

She frowned, but stood up to move to the sofa anyway, feeling a sense of surprise as he sat next to her, his thighs almost touching hers. Almost ... That made her more aware of him than ever! 'Do I need to be more comfortable?' she asked lightly.

He grimaced. 'For what I have to say, yes, I think so.'

Morgan instantly tensed. 'It sounds ominous.'

'I'm hoping not,' he said dryly. 'My talk concerns Courtney.'

'Of course.' Now why should she feel disappointment in that? Courtney was the only reason she was in England. Wasn't he . . .?

'Although my problem of solving the problem is unorthodox,' he added reluctantly.

'Courtney is a little young for boarding-school,' she derided.

There was no answering smile from Alex, just a renewed tightening of his mouth. 'I don't plan to send him to boarding-school—ever,' he bit out.

Morgan's eyes widened. 'I thought all you Hammonds went to boarding-school?' she frowned.

'We did,' he growled. 'Which is precisely the reason I would never send a child of mine to one.'

She stiffened. 'Courtney isn't your child.'

'Not yet,' he acknowledged softly. 'But I plan for him to be. And I think you should be his mother.'

She swallowed hard. 'What do you mean?'

Alex shrugged, staring into the fire. 'You obviously love the baby very much. And I think those reporters may have come up with the solution to our problem.' He turned intense grey eyes on her. 'I think we should get married.'

Morgan stared at him with widely shocked eyes, the pupils dilating in her surprise. *Marry* Alex Hammond? That wasn't unorthodox, that was ridiculous!

'I can see the idea surprises you,' he drawled derisively. 'But I can see no other solution. I refuse to give Courtney up, and so do you, and unless we want him to become a child who's tugged from one side of the Atlantic to the other on a six-monthly basis I don't see what else we can do.'

'But my work is in the States.' It was the first objection that came to mind—but not the only one!

Alex looked grim. 'You enjoy your career?'

'I—Yes.'

'Then we'll have to find a way round that.' He frowned thoughtfully. 'I could always move the Hammond head office to the States so that Courtney and I could be with you.'

'No! I mean—You would really do that?' she asked incredulously, knowing by the seriousness of the suggestion that he was in deadly earnest about marrying her.

He nodded. 'If I have no other choice. Courtney has to come first.'

'And what about you?' she queried breathlessly. 'Don't you want to marry a woman you love?' She looked at him with tense curiosity; his answer to this was suddenly important to her.

His mouth twisted, the grey eyes cold. 'Love is a destructive emotion. It tends to leave the people who really love with no will of their own, completely vulnerable to the other person's whims. No,' he met her gaze steadily, 'I have no wish to be destroyed in that way. Ours would be a marriage of convenience——'

'That went out with the Victorians!' Morgan snapped, deeply confused by his views on love. He must have loved—and lost—someone once, someone who took advantage of his love instead of treasuring it.

'I didn't say it would be platonic,' Alex drawled. 'I have no intention of living the rest of my life celibate. I have had—relationships, in the past. You didn't find my kisses unpleasant this afternoon, I'm sure you wouldn't find me unsatisfactory in bed.'

She knew she must have flushed, despite the veneer of sophistication she had acquired as an actress. She just didn't expect Alex Hammond to talk to her in this intimate way. 'I'm sure I wouldn't,' she acknowledged brittly, knowing this man would be successful at everything he did—including making love! 'But I can't marry you.'

'Why not?' That probing grey gaze swept over the confusion of her face. 'You told me you have no intention of marrying this man Sam you've been seeing. Just think of me as a lifetime affair rather than a fleeting one. I can assure you I wouldn't force myself on you more than necessary,' he added at her gasp of indignation. 'I enjoy women, when in the mood, but if necessary I can control my sexual urges to a minimum.'

She couldn't take this in, couldn't accept what was so calmly being said to her. 'Let me get this straight,' she said tautly. 'I marry you, we live—wherever, provide Courtney with parents, and occasionally you make the trip from your bedroom to mine?'

'The latter would be a two-way thing,' he told her arrogantly. 'Women have desires and needs too, I'm aware of that.'

'So if I want a man I just come over to your bedroom?' Her eyes sparkled deeply green in her anger.

Alex shrugged. 'What's wrong with that?'

'Nothing—if you happen to be a damned machine!' she snapped furiously. 'What you're proposing is inhuman!'

His frown of puzzlement seemed genuine. 'I don't see it that way.'

'That's obvious!'

He sighed. 'Look, if you're worried I won't be able to give you a fulfilling physical relationship I can always show you now that you're wrong.'

Morgan backed away from him, from the cold determination in his face. 'This is no way to make love . . .' she told him weakly as he pushed her gently back against the cushions.

'Perhaps we won't make love now,' he agreed. 'Although I think I should show you that we could physically give each other pleasure.'

'You're so clinical!' She pushed ineffectually against his chest as he bent over her.

'I can be less so,' he promised throatily. 'You're very beautiful, Morgan. Let me show you how good it could be between us.'

It wasn't a case of 'letting' him do anything—she couldn't stop him! Maybe if her emotions hadn't already been heightened by the trauma of the day she might have been able to stop him—and maybe she wouldn't! At the first touch of his lips that now familiar languor swept over her body, and she was powerless to resist anything he did.

He kissed her with long drugging movements of his mouth, devouring her, drawing her into him so that she had no thoughts but those of pleasing him and being pleasured by him in return.

And he did pleasure her, slowly moving the zip of her gown down her spine, pushing the soft black material off her shoulder, exposing pert pink-tipped breasts to his avid mouth. He didn't take the hardened nipple completely into his mouth, teasing it with the warm moistness of his tongue until she groaned with needing more than that, then he left that breast to the pleasure-giving ministrations of his fingertips, his mouth moving in slow hot kisses between the valley of her breasts to the other waiting nipple.

She gasped at the sudden sucking on the taut bud, the teasing bites of his teeth as she arched against him, her fingers intwined in the darkness of his hair as she held him to her. She was completely under his sexual domination, and knew by the tautness of his thighs that her body aroused him in return. But it wasn't enough for her, she wanted him to be more than aroused by her body, wanted him to shake under her caresses too, to know that as a woman she pleased him.

With a slight shift in their positions on the sofa she was able to be slightly above him, and so in the dominant position herself, her breasts still knowing the fevered caresses of his lips and tongue. She felt him stiffen as she began to slip the jacket from his shoulders, and then he relaxed, sitting up slightly to help her take it off completely, his mouth nuzzling her throat now, biting erotically into her earlobe.

She quivered in reaction, squirming against him, her hands shaking as she slowly unbuttoned his shirt, loving the muscled hardness revealed to her caressing fingers. Her mouth kissed and tasted every area of his chest, teasing the male nipples in the same way he had caressed her, feeling him shudder in response.

He gasped. 'No woman has ever—How did you know——'

She smiled down at him in satisfaction. 'Intuition,' she murmured throatily.

'Do you know any other—intuitive caresses like that?' he groaned, a high flush of sexual pleasure to his lean cheeks.

'I'll make them up as I go along,' she promised against the tautness of his hard stomach.

And she did. Her caresses were all instinctive; she had never known the full intimacy of a man's body before, but found she loved the barely leashed control of Alex's, making no protest as he again took over, kneeling beside the sofa as he slipped her dress off completely, only her black lacy panties covering her nakedness now.

'You're perfect!' Alex groaned as he covered her body with his, one hand caressing the firm curve of her hips, slipping knowledgeably beneath the lace to find the centre of her passion.

His caresses knew no bounds now, and Morgan

groaned into the warmth of his mouth as her desire threatened to spiral out of control, flicking her tongue enticingly along the edge of his lips as she pleaded for an end to his tortuous caresses. Alex's mouth opened against hers, and he groaned, his thighs surging wildly against hers.

Moments later he was pulling roughly away from her, breathing deeply. 'We have to stop now,' he said raggedly.

'No . . .!' She gave a moan of sexual frustration. 'Alex, please!' She clung to him in appeal.

'Do you think I don't want you too?' He held her arms at her sides. 'You know I do!' he groaned. 'But not here, and not like this.' His eyes were a smoky grey colour as he slowly regained control of himself. 'And I don't think we should cloud the situation with a physical relationship.'

'But you just said——'

'I know what I said.' He swung away from her, standing up, pulling on his shirt but making no move to fasten it. 'I've changed my mind. We've just proved that, physically, we're compatible. We don't need to go any further to know that. Agreed?'

Her own control was slower in coming, the rapid rise and fall of her breasts evidence of that. But the way Alex couldn't even bring himself to look at her, staring down at the dying embers of the fire, was like a cold shower on her emotions, and she pulled her dress back into place, feeling a return of some of her dignity along with it. 'Agreed,' she said curtly. 'I wouldn't want to *cloud* the situation,' she added tautly.

Alex did turn now. 'Morgan——'

'I can't marry you, Alex——'

'You haven't even thought about it!'

'I don't need to,' she spoke calmly. 'It wouldn't work, Alex. All the problems that made Glenna so unhappy would apply to me too if I were your wife.'

'What problems?' he bit out savagely.

Just to look at him unnerved her, his dark hair still ruffled from her caressing fingers, his tanned hair-roughened chest still aching to be touched. She wasn't aware of her own tousled hair, her lips bare of lip-gloss, still swollen with the passion that had raged through her minutes earlier. 'Your mother, living here, the fact that England is not my native country. We don't even have love between us to help make it work.'

'Granted,' he acknowledged curtly. 'But that's precisely the reason I think it would work. My mother is *my* problem, not yours. And you haven't seemed as if you dislike England while you've been here. Besides, you'll still have your career.'

She frowned her puzzlement. 'I can still work?'

'Of course,' he replied, as if he had never considered she would do anything else. 'If the character of Mary-Beth is completely acting, as you say it is, then you're too good to stop.'

Morgan flushed at the taunt. 'You might be surprised,' she snapped. 'But have you considered the fact that if I continued with the series I'd be in the States for six months of the—Ah,' she gave him an accusing glare. 'I understand now. If I marry you Courtney stays here all the time, but *I* leave for six months every year. No way, Alex!'

He looked down his nose at her with haughty arrogance. 'I believe I told you I would make the move to the States if that's what you want. I want to provide a stable background for Courtney, at any price.'

Her anger turned to confusion. He meant it about moving to the States, she could see that in the determination of his expression. She only had to say the word and he would leave this house and move his business to the States. She couldn't ask that of him, and no matter how much she disliked Rita Hammond she couldn't do it to the other woman either. The other woman had already lost one son; to lose her other one, and her only grandson, was likely to break even the hardened Rita Hammond.

'Don't think about it now,' Alex encouraged softly as he sensed her uncertainty. 'Go back to the States tomorrow, think about it while you're away. There's no rush, a few weeks isn't going to make any difference. And I believe it's something you do need to think about.'

'*You* didn't,' she pointed out softly.

'Not for long, no,' he admitted. 'But then it's different for me, I have nothing to lose by marrying you.'

'Your freedom?'

His mouth twisted derisively. 'That isn't so much. And I would be gaining so much more, a beautiful wife, a healthy son.'

Morgan blushed at the compliment. 'It really does need thinking about, Alex.'

'Take all the time you need. I won't rush you.'

The thinking began that night, to such an extreme that she hardly slept. She looked at Alex's idea from every angle, and every time she came up with the same answer. But it was an answer she didn't want. America was her home, with Sam as her boy-friend, and her parents not too far away; she didn't need a complicated man like Alex Hammond in her life. He had the depths of no man she had ever met before!

She almost turned and ran when she entered the dining-room the next morning to find only Rita Hammond there. The other woman took great pleasure in telling her that Alex had already eaten and was in his study doing some last-minute work before driving her to the airport.

'But it gives us a chance to talk alone,' Rita Hammond added warningly.

Morgan instantly stiffened, deciding coffee was all she could stomach this morning if the other woman was going to start being insulting.

'What did Alex want to talk to you about last night?'

Her eyes widened at this open attack—talk about straight for the jugular! 'He didn't tell you?' she prevaricated.

Rita shot her a vehement look. 'I would hardly be asking if that were the case. Alex has always been a—solitary person. I have no doubt he'll tell me, in time.'

'But you'd rather not wait?' Morgan derided.

'No,' Rita agreed tautly.

Morgan drew in a deep breath, sipping her coffee slowly. 'I can't tell you either, Mrs Hammond,' she gave the only answer she could in the circumstances. 'If Alex had wanted you to know he would have told you. I'm afraid you'll just have to wait until he decides to tell you.'

The other woman's face became an ugly mask in her anger. 'Don't get clever with me on the basis of one kiss, Morgan!' she rasped. 'A little comforting got out of hand, I refuse to believe it was any more than that!'

'Believe away,' she shrugged dismissively. 'I can't add to that.'

'You don't need to,' Rita scorned. 'I have more faith in Alex than to believe he would become seriously involved with a woman like you.'

'That will be enough!' Alex spoke coldly from the doorway behind them. 'I will not have you insulting Morgan any more, Mother,' he added tautly.

'But——'

'I'm ready to leave for the airport now if you are, Morgan,' he cut across his mother's protest.

She gave him a grateful smile and stood up. 'I just have to say goodbye to Courtney.'

'He'll hardly know anything about it,' the older

woman derided, still pale from her son's anger with her.

'And it isn't goodbye,' Alex added softly.

'It isn't?' his mother demanded sharply, forgetting to be wary of his biting tongue in her surprise.

He looked at her with chilling grey eyes. 'Morgan intends returning to us in a few weeks' time,' he informed her.

'I didn't know that,' his mother flushed.

'Oh, Morgan always intended to return, she has Courtney's future to think of. Doesn't she?' He looked at Morgan challengingly.

Her gaze was caught and held by his. 'I do,' she acknowledged softly. 'I'm just not sure what it's going to be yet,' she added the last for him alone.

'I told you, there's no hurry,' he soothed gently.

She knew that he was just assuring her that he hadn't changed his mind since last night, and she was grateful for that. She had finally drifted off to sleep about four o'clock this morning, waking with a start what seemed like minutes later, sure that she must have dreamt it all, that Alex Hammond hadn't really asked her to marry him. This man was too perceptive; he had been able to read her uncertainty so easily. And he had reassured her as easily. There was no mistake, he meant every word he had said last night.

'What's going on here?' Rita Hammond cut in sharply. 'Alex, I want to know what's happening between the two of you?'

His brows rose arrogantly at the demand. 'Nothing is "happening" at the moment, Mother,' he told her coldly. 'And even if it were I consider it no one's business but Morgan's and my own. If there is ever anything I think you should know about us you can be sure I'll tell you. In the meantime, Morgan and I have to leave,' and he swept Morgan from the room with his hand firmly on her arm.

'Whew!' she breathed a sigh of relief once they were out in the hallway, smiling up at Alex. 'I don't know how you dare talk to her like that.'

'Practice,' he drawled abruptly, with no answering humour in his harsh features. 'Hurry and see Courtney,' he glanced at the plain gold watch on his wrist. 'We don't have long to get to the airport.'

It broke Morgan's heart to say goodbye to the baby, and as if he knew she was going away he began to cry, his little face all red in his distress.

'It won't be long,' she kissed his cheeks, feeling like crying herself, 'I promise, baby.'

'Don't make promises you can't keep,' Alex warned as he came into the room.

She looked up at him, nuzzling against the baby's red curls. 'Oh, I'll keep it this time. I just don't know if I'll be staying after that.'

'We really should be going, Morgan,' he prompted gently. 'I have to go into the office after I've taken you to the airport.'

'Sorry,' she mumbled, and put the baby back in his crib. 'I'm ready.' She set her mouth bravely, turning and walking out of the room without a second glance.

Her control lasted until they were actually on their way to the airport, when the resounding cry of Courtney from upstairs as she left the house couldn't be denied any longer. Oh, she was going to miss the baby!

'I know,' Alex's hand came out to clasp hers. 'He's going to miss you too.'

'Will he?' she choked. 'Will he really?'

'I'm sure he will,' he consoled gently. 'You underestimate his understanding of your love.'

'Mrs Ford said something along the same lines,' Morgan admitted.

'I told you she's a good nurse.'

'There's no need to look so smug!' She pulled her

hand away from his. 'I'll admit Mrs Ford has turned out to be very nice. But she's going to have to leave eventually, then what happens to Courtney?'

Alex shrugged broad shoulders beneath the charcoal grey suit and silver-grey shirt. 'That's a decision we'll both have to make when the time comes.'

He made it sound as if it were already taken for granted that they were a couple, that they were used to making decisions together. And in a way they were going to be, for even if she didn't marry Alex they would still remain joint guardians of Courtney until he was eighteen.

Los Angeles looked the same smoggy, beautiful city Morgan had come to love during the last two years of living and working here. It felt good to be back, and she ran into Sam's arms as he met her at the airport, kissing him enthusiastically.

'Bad, huh?' he sympathised, his arm about her shoulders as they left the airport together.

'In parts,' she nodded. 'Can we not talk about it, Sam? Not yet.'

'Okay, honey.' He held her tightly against his side. 'Whenever you're ready.'

'Tell me how work's going,' she prompted instead.

'The usual.' He went on to tell her all the studio gossip. 'I think they're waiting to see what your reaction is to signing another contract before they decide what to do with Mary-Beth at the end of the season. There's been a rumour that you don't want to stay on.' He gave her a sideways glance as they drove to her apartment.

She turned to grin at him. 'That's no rumour, Sam, I told Jerry myself weeks ago I didn't think I would be interested.'

'It's your decision, sweetheart,' he shrugged.

Sam's lack of forcefulness, his way of respecting her

opinions and wishes, had always appealed to her in the past, and yet right now she could have done with more than a little help in this most important decision of her life. But she couldn't talk about it with Sam, not at all.

She made the trip to her parents' house the next day, shocked to see how ill her father still looked, despite being out of hospital for several days. Glenna's death had hit him harder than it had any of them.

'I want to see my grandson,' he growled, sitting out on the sun-deck of the house, the pallor of illness still with him as he looked almost frail.

'A couple of months before you can even think about flying, the doctor said,' Morgan's mother put in lightly.

'What do they know?' he muttered.

'Well, *I* know you aren't well enough.' Once again her mother was the one being strong—and doing it very well too!

'Tell me what he looks like again, Morgan,' her father pleaded.

Throughout the day she must have told her father half a dozen times what Courtney looked like, the little things he did, but she told her father all over again, never tiring of talking about the baby herself.

'He should be called Court, not Courtney,' her father roared. 'What sort of name is that for a boy?'

'Yours,' she pointed out gently.

'And of course the Hammonds have to carry it out to the letter,' he scorned.

'Of course,' she agreed laughingly. 'Alex insisted.'

'I must say he's always been very polite when we've spoken to him on the telephone,' her mother gave her a searching look.

'Politeness costs nothing,' her father snapped. 'Especially to a Hammond. Think they own the damned world! Well, I want my grandson here where he belongs,' he pinpointed Morgan with eyes as green as her own. 'You should have brought him with you.'

'He's too young to fly all that way, Dad. Especially being premature.'

'Well, as soon as he's old enough I want him out here.'

She avoided his gaze, chewing on her bottom lip. 'That might be a little difficult, Dad. You see, Alex is determined Courtney will stay with him.'

'And who's he, to dictate where my grandson goes?' her father demanded. 'Glenna should never—should never have——' to Morgan's consternation he began to cry.

It was a heartrending experience for her to see this strong man cry. In all the years she could remember she could never recall her father having cried about anything before, not even when his own father had died a couple of years ago.

She watched with tears in her own eyes as her mother helped him through the house to their bedroom, and she was still sitting in the armchair when her mother returned a few minutes later.

'Losing Glenna like that has been very hard on him,' her mother explained gently. 'Knowing about Courtney is what's kept him going.'

'I know.' Morgan dried her cheeks. 'And I will bring him over here, as soon as I can.'

'And what will Alex Hammond have to say to that?'

She turned away. Alex would agree to her bringing Courtney to America on only one condition, she knew that. 'He—I think he'll be agreeable.'

The work schedule was such over the next week that Morgan hardly had time to sleep, let alone dwell on the unconscious decision she had made concerning Alex's proposal. She continued to see Sam when their work schedules would allow it, and on the eve of her departure back to England they had dinner together at his beach-house.

'When will you be back this time?' he queried casually.

She smiled, lazing on the warm golden sand in the last of the evening's sunshine. 'Jerry has given me only a couple of days this time—no more than that,' she successfully mimicked the director's voice. 'Then it's back for the last two weeks of filming,' she spoke in her own voice.

'And after that?'

She chewed on her bottom lip. 'I was hoping you wouldn't ask me that.'

He looked at her steadily, very bronzed in his dark swimming trunks. 'Why not?'

'Because I—I don't think I'm coming back after that.'

He couldn't hide his start of surprise. 'I don't understand,' he frowned. 'You don't mean to stay in England indefinitely?'

'I—could.' She gave an indecisive shrug. 'I'm really not sure yet.'

'Is there anything I can do to persuade you to stay? Since Joanie died I've been very lonely,' he told her softly. 'The last few months you've helped fill that loneliness.'

She squeezed his hand as it lay on the sand beside her. 'I'm glad of that. You're a wonderful man, Sam. You deserve to be happy.'

'But not with you?' His gaze was intent.

She gave a rueful shake of her head. 'I don't think so. I've enjoyed being with you, in fact, I've loved every moment of it. But perhaps that's half the trouble,' she realised thoughtfully. 'Love isn't all joy—Glenna's marriage showed me that. What do they call it in books, the agony and the ecstasy?'

'It was like that with Joanie,' he admitted huskily.

'And me?' she prompted softly, knowing that she hadn't reached either the high or the low with Sam, that enjoying his company just wasn't enough. Alex had shown her the ecstasy at least.

'Well. I——'

'I know it wasn't, Sam,' she said gently. 'Not for you or for me. We've had fun, let's leave it at that.'

'Did you meet the man here or in England? England, of course,' he answered his own question. 'Otherwise you wouldn't be going to stay there.'

Morgan frowned. 'What man?'

'The one who showed you the agony and the ecstasy, the man you're in love with.'

Colour flooded her cheeks. 'I don't love him!' Alex Hammond wasn't a lovable man. He was desirable, extremely so, but he wasn't lovable.

'No?' Sam asked sceptically.

'No,' she insisted firmly.

No, she didn't love Alex, but she was going to marry him. This last week without Courtney had shown her that he was as much a part of her as if she had actually brought him into the world. And her physical reaction to Alex couldn't be dismissed either; she had longed to know that pleasure again since she had been away from him. And then there was her father. She couldn't bear the recrimination in his eyes if she should ever lose Courtney to Alex in a legal battle. Marriage was the only answer, but with a few changes to the arrangements Alex had suggested. She wondered how he was going to react to them.

CHAPTER FIVE

HER nervousness grew as the plane touched down at Heathrow, and she felt herself become even more tense as she took a cab from the airport to the Hammond home. No doubt Alex would have either sent a car or come for her himself if he had known when she was arriving. But she hadn't told him, preferring to arrive in her own time, at her own pace, not intending to relinquish one particle of her independence even when she was his wife.

Symonds was no more welcoming than the last time, informing her that Rita Hammond was at her daughter's for the evening, and that Alex hadn't arrived home from his office yet. Well, at least with Rita out of the house she was going to be able to meet and talk to Alex in privacy.

The butler showed her into the same bedroom as before, informing her that dinner would be served in one hour. That suited Morgan perfectly, as she wanted to see Courtney before she showered and changed for dinner.

The baby was as adorable as ever, and she spent so much time with him, amazed at how much he had changed in just that one week, that she almost forgot to change for dinner. In the end she needn't have made the effort.

'Mr Alex telephoned several minutes ago, Miss McKay,' Symonds told her haughtily. 'He was intending to stay in London overnight, but when I told him you had arrived unexpectedly he changed his plans. He told me to inform you he will be home some time this evening, although a business meeting could delay him.'

'Thank you,' she accepted dully, although not by the flicker of an eyelid did she show her disappointment as she ate her dinner alone. She had expected to talk to Alex this evening, had prepared herself for it, now she doubted they would be able to say more than goodnight to each other!

As it turned out they didn't even get to do that! After the delicious meal she was given, and the wine Symonds had insisted had to be served with it, she became very drowsy, the jet-lag catching up with her with a vengeance. By ten-thirty Alex hadn't returned from London—and Morgan was safely tucked up in bed, fast asleep!

'Why are you here?' Rita Hammond demanded of her the next morning, once again only the two of them in the dining-room for breakfast.

'You knew I was coming back,' she shrugged, wondering where Alex was, and not wanting to get into an argument with this woman.

'Oh I knew, I just don't understand why.' Rita Hammond looked at her with open dislike. 'Why don't you just leave Courtney with us, and stop trying to pull him in two? He'll hate you for it in the end, you know.'

She did know; it had been another of the deciding factors in her decision, that and the attraction she and Alex undoubtedly had for each other. 'Has Alex eaten already?' she changed the subject.

'He isn't here,' the other woman took great delight in telling her. 'He hasn't been here all night.'

'His business appointment must have kept him very late,' Morgan frowned.

'Business appointment? Is that what Symonds told you it was?' Rita scorned. 'Well, no doubt that's what Alex told him to say,' she gave a derisive smile. 'Alex does not stay in London overnight on business,' she added pointedly.

Morgan stood up jerkily. 'If you'll excuse me,' she said tautly, 'I still have some unpacking to do.'

Rita Hammond watched her contemptuously. 'How long do you intend honouring us with your presence this time?'

'Only until tomorrow,' she snapped, her eyes flashing deeply green.

'I'm sure Alex will return before you leave. Let's hope we will have seen the last of the McKay family then,' she added with dislike.

'I don't wish to discuss that with you,' Morgan dismissed.

'My son has been giving me the same reply all week,' the other woman bit out. 'I suppose that when he's ready he'll speak to me about whatever is troubling him.'

'I'm sure he will,' Morgan evaded, and made good her escape.

She spent the morning with Courtney, all the time waiting for Alex's return. His mother's pointed hints had told her that Alex had been with a woman last night and not on business at all, and she felt jealousy rip through her at the thought of another woman knowing his caresses, his drugging kisses. She knew it was ridiculous of her, unreasonable, and yet she couldn't fight her feelings of jealousy. She didn't even love the man, and she felt jealousy of his making love to another woman!

She heard the Mercedes in the driveway mid-afternoon, and looked down from her bedroom to see Alex swinging agilely out from behind the wheel of the car, dark and forceful in a navy blue suit, the grey in his hair more noticeable as the light breeze ruffled it into disorder.

For a disconcerting moment she felt an urge to run down to him and throw herself in his arms! But she didn't. She heard his mother greet him and then the sound of a door slamming. He must know she was here, and yet he had made no effort to see her! Had he changed his mind about wanting to marry her after all?

She turned sharply as a knock sounded lightly on her bedroom door, and called out for the person to come in. Her breath caught in her throat as Alex came into the room; the person slamming the door must have been his mother.

'I—How are you?' Morgan suddenly felt shy—which was ridiculous for a twenty-six-year-old woman! None of her friends in Los Angeles would believe how Alex affected her, how just to look at him made her knees weak.

'I'm fine.' He came in and closed the door, feeling no awkwardness himself. 'You've seen Courtney?'

'I've spent the morning with him,' she nodded.

'Evading my mother,' he derided.

'Partly,' she admitted, tall and elegant in a navy blue blouse and white skirt. 'But mainly because I just wanted to be with him.'

Alex nodded. 'I'm sorry I didn't get back last night. I had an important meeting that went on until after twelve, and when I telephoned the house Symonds said you'd been in bed for two hours. I decided it would be simpler to drive down today.'

'Of course.' She evaded his gaze.

Grey eyes narrowed. 'You were told I was delayed, weren't you?'

'I'm afraid I fell asleep last night, as Symonds told you. Your mother told me this morning that you hadn't come back yet.'

'Then——' he broke off, heaving a deep sigh. 'Let's forget about that. Shall we talk now or later?'

The directness of his question unnerved her, all her carefully rehearsed speeches were forgotten. 'Er—later, I think,' she heard herself say. 'I'm sure you'd much rather freshen up now.'

He ran a hand around the back of his tired nape. 'I would,' he agreed wearily. 'I had a rough time last night.'

'I'm sure,' she agreed tightly.

Alex nodded. 'I never sleep well in hotels.'

'Hotels——?' she frowned. 'You stayed in a hotel last night?' Somehow she hadn't been expecting that, had thought he would stay at the woman's home, Unless . . .? Goodness, she had been taken in by Rita Hammond so easily!

'Mm,' Alex grimaced. 'And I didn't get to bed until almost two o'clock. I'm having trouble with one of my companies up north. The union had the impression— But you don't want to hear this,' he shook his head ruefully.

After the fool she had almost made of herself Morgan was very curious to know the real reason for his delay in London. 'But I do,' she prompted eagerly. 'Please—tell me about it.'

He shrugged. 'My work-force up there were just a little concerned I might be closing the company down. And when the unions get hold of something like that they don't want to let go. I had to drive up there this morning and reassure them in person. Damned nonsense!'

'And I thought—Never mind what I thought,' she dismissed hastily as she saw his eyes narrow. 'We can talk whenever you want to,' she added brightly.

'Later will be fine,' he told her absently, his expression tight. 'Just where did you think I was last night?'

'In London, of course,' she replied awkwardly.

His eyes became flinty now. 'But not alone, hmm?'

She chewed on her bottom lip. 'No,' she admitted abruptly.

Alex's head went back arrogantly. 'If I'd spent the night in London with a woman I would have made no secret of it. I don't happen to have a mistress in London. I don't have a mistress *anywhere*,' he added derisively.

Morgan's fingers were laced tightly together. 'I'm sorry,' she mumbled.

'Would you like a list of the relationships I've had for the last five years?' he rasped.

He was really angry, and she couldn't exactly blame him. 'I said I was sorry, Alex,' she pleaded. 'It's just that Symonds said you were coming back last night.' She didn't want to involve his mother in this.

'I was delayed—I've just explained that,' he bit out.

Morgan swallowed hard, realising how ridiculous this conversation was even if he didn't. 'You don't ave to explain anything to me, Alex. I made an ssumption,' with a lot of help from Rita Hammond! 'and I've apologised for it. I wish we could just drop the subject now.' She had no intention of telling him of his mother's deliberate lie; she knew she should have had more sense than to listen to the other woman. Because she did believe Alex, knew he wasn't a man who lied. Rita Hammond would feel no such compunction.

'Then we will,' he agreed curtly. 'I'll just go and see Courtney and then take a shower. We'll talk in my study after dinner.'

Her cheeks coloured fiery red as she remembered what had happened the last time they went to the study to talk. Alex's mocking glance told her he remembered it too.

She chastised herself once he had gone to his own room. What a fool she had been to listen to his mother! And how gullibly she had behaved. If Rita Hammond had chipped away at Glenna and Mark's marriage in the same way no wonder they had run into difficulty; Mark's defence of his mother had been much stronger than Alex's.

She was polite but cool with the other woman as they all dined together that evening. She knew by the triumphant glitter in icy blue eyes that Rita Hammond considered she had scored a minor victory this morning by planting those seeds of doubt in Morgan's mind. And maybe she had, but in future Morgan would know to be more wary of the woman.

Morgan could see the other woman's curiosity was aroused as she and Alex once more retired to his study, but neither of them offered an explanation for going.

Alex seated himself behind the desk this time, at once putting them on a businesslike footing. His gaze was intent on her composed features. 'Did you come to a decision while you were away?'

This time she was ready for his directness, and she answered calmly. 'Yes, I did.'

Something flickered in his eyes and then faded. He sighed. 'I can understand your saying no, you don't even know me, and it would be a lifetime commitment to a stranger.' He stood up to pace the room. 'A life without love and——'

'I'm not going to say no, Alex,' she put in softly.

He turned to face her sharply, his eyes narrowing. 'You aren't?'

'No.'

'Why not?'

She gave a mocking smile at his surprise. 'I must say you aren't being very flattering when I've just accepted your proposal of marriage,' she taunted.

He ran a hand through the thick darkness of his hair. 'It's unexpected——'

'Don't you want me to marry you?'

'Of course,' he said stiffly.

'Don't you consider yourself eligible?' she mocked.

'I've never thought about it!'

'Then you should. I accept your proposal, Alex. I'll marry you.' She was coolly composed.

He blinked. 'When?'

She shrugged. 'As soon as my work in America has finished, I suppose.'

'Very well,' he moved to sit behind the desk once more, 'I'll make all the arrangements——'

'I haven't finished yet, Alex,' she interrupted softly. 'I'll accept your proposal with certain changes made in the agreement.'

'Yes?' He was wary now.

Morgan laughed softly and stood up, very slender in a dark bottle-green dress that made her hair look like a flame, her eyes deeper in the reflected colour. 'Don't look so worried, Alex,' she taunted. 'I'm not going to ask you to sign over the family fortune to me.'

'Mary-Beth would,' he derided.

Her mouth twisted. 'If Mary-Beth threatened *you* I have a feeling she'd come to a nasty end,' she grimaced. 'My first change is that I won't be in *Power Trap* after this season. I've asked to be written out of it, and the producers have agreed.'

'You're giving up your career?' he frowned.

'Yes,' she nodded. 'For now, at least. Courtney needs a full-time mother, not a part-time one. That's another change I would like to make.' She looked at him challengingly.

Alex sat back in his chair with a look of resigned expectation. 'Yes?' he prompted.

'I want to take care of the baby myself, no nanny. Yes, Alex,' she insisted as he went to protest. 'Mrs Ford will be leaving soon, and I do know how to look after Courtney.'

'I don't doubt it,' he said gently. 'It's just that caring for a baby is a big responsibility, a twenty-four hour a day job.'

'One I shall love. I'll make a deal with you, Alex,' she told him. 'If after a month you don't think I can cope you can get him a nanny. How's that?'

He sighed. 'By the confidence in your voice I would say it's a one-sided deal. Okay,' he gave a rueful shrug, 'if that's what you really want.'

'It is,' she nodded. 'Now I come to the last change I want to make.'

'There's more?' he groaned.

She swallowed hard. 'Yes. I—This part could be a little embarrassing,' she chewed on her bottom lip.

His icy gaze searched her face, his mouth tightening. 'I understand,' he bit out abruptly. 'You would rather we didn't have a physical relationship,' he sighed. 'I'm a little sceptical that a marriage can work without it, but I——'

'Alex, you have it all wrong again,' she told him impatiently. 'Stop jumping to conclusions.'

'Sorry!'

She smiled at his sarcasm. 'I'm arguing with you again, aren't I?'

'Yes,' he sighed.

'I don't mean to. I just want you to listen to me.' She straightened her shoulders. 'I want you, Alex. I want you very badly.' She saw the ruddy hue colour his cheeks. 'I've thought of nothing else but you since I went away. I want to be your wife, Alex, but not as a part-time lover. I want to share a bedroom with you, not have to make a trip across a corridor or through a connecting door.' She gave a half smile. 'If I did that every time I wanted to spend the night with you the carpet between our two rooms would be worn away!' she attempted to joke.

He cleared his throat, obviously unnerved by her bluntness. 'I—You——'

She gave a self-derisive laugh. 'Now I've embarrassed you. And I didn't mean to,' she sighed. 'But I've never felt this way before, never wanted a man the way I want you. I wanted to be honest about the attraction, that's all.'

'I'm not embarrassed,' he dismissed. 'A little surprised perhaps, but not really embarrassed. Did you see Sam while you were away?'

She frowned at the unexpectedness of the question. 'Yes . . .'

'And that didn't change the desire you feel for me?'

'No,' she answered instantly.

He turned away, staring down into the fireplace. 'If we're dealing in honesty I think I should tell you I feel that electricity between us too. I've tried to push it to the back of my mind the last few days, but I haven't been able to forget the feel or taste of you. What I'm trying to say is that I share your need, that I'd like to protect the carpet at all costs,' he made an attempt to lighten the tension that suddenly filled the room. But it didn't work, the electricity sparking a fire between them. 'Morgan . . .!' he groaned.

She went into his arms willingly, meeting the hunger in him with one of her own, kissing and touching him as fiercely as he touched her.

'Will you come to my room with me now?' he groaned raggedly. 'I need you!'

She wanted to—she could imagine nothing more ecstatic than spending the night in his arms, in his bed. And yet she held back from that final commitment, wanting her wedding night to be the first time she knew his full possession.

'No?' He sensed her reserve, and pulled back, the flush of passion to his cheeks. 'Are you just like all women after all, I wonder?' he rasped. 'You admitted wanting me, but that admission drew one from me in return,' his mouth twisted. 'I'll never be controlled by the use of a physical attraction, Morgan,' he snapped, pushing her fully away from him. 'No woman's body is worth losing even one ounce of self-respect or self-control.'

He spoke with an inner bitterness that caused

Morgan pain—because he spoke from personal experience! Now she knew the reason for his aloofness, his solitariness. There had once been a woman in his life, a woman he loved, who had used her body to blackmail him in the relationship. Only time would show him that she wasn't like that, that she was as weakened by wanting him as he would be in wanting her.

'I accept all your conditions, Morgan,' he rasped coldly, distant from her now. 'I'll inform my mother of our marriage in the morning.'

At least she would be spared the other woman's wrath for one more night. But what about Alex's coldness? She put out a hand to him. 'Alex——'

He evaded that hand without being too pointed about it. 'I have some work to do now,' he dismissed abruptly.

She nodded. 'I shall be free of all commitments in America in two weeks' time. I——'

'Does that include Sam?' His eyes were glacial.

'Of course,' she flashed. 'I intend being a faithful wife, Alex. You may do what you please.'

His hand was painful on her arm as he swung her round roughly to face him. 'I shall be faithful to you for as long as it takes for you to tire of being a wife and mother and look for other amusements,' he ground out fiercely.

Morgan's head was back proudly. 'I don't envisage that ever happening,' she bit out tautly.

His mouth twisted derisively before he released her. 'We shall see.'

'I'm sure we shall,' she nodded. 'I'll leave you now if you want to work. I leave tomorrow evening, by the way. I'm afraid your mother is going to be disappointed when she knows I'm coming back—to stay this time,' she mocked.

'I would say the likelihood of my mother having

hysterics when I tell her we intend marrying is about a hundred per cent,' Alex drawled.

'You don't sound concerned.'

His expression was arrogant. 'My choice of bride is no one's affair but my own.'

'But you know I'm the last choice she would make for you!'

'I'm way beyond asking my mother's permission for anything I do,' he snapped. 'She may say what she likes, do what she likes, but I intend marrying you in two weeks' time.'

'As soon as I get back?' Morgan gasped.

He raised dark brows. 'Is there any reason for us to wait longer than that?'

'None at all,' she replied tautly. 'My father still isn't well enough to travel, no matter when we marry.'

'We could be married from your home if you would prefer.'

She frowned. 'You would do that?'

'If it's what you want,' he nodded.

'But Courtney——'

'Is not coming on our honeymoon with us,' he dismissed hardly. 'Mrs Ford can stay on and take care of him until we get back.'

'We're going on a honeymoon?'

'I believe it's traditional,' he taunted. 'I thought Barbados for a couple of weeks. We could visit your parents on our way there if you would prefer that.'

Rita Hammond was going to have enough reason to dislike her without denying the woman the opportunity to have her eldest son married in England. 'I think that's a better idea,' she agreed.

'Very well,' he nodded distantly, dismissively.

The coldness of his expression wasn't very encouraging, but Morgan remained undeterred, reaching up on tiptoe to kiss him lingeringly on the lips. 'Goodnight, Alex,' she murmured throatily. 'I *will* make you happy,' she vowed.

He made no reply, but went to sit behind his desk, taking some papers out of his briefcase, concluding the conversation.

Morgan went slowly up to her room. The woman in Alex's past had hurt him very badly, had used the attraction he felt for her as a weapon against him. She couldn't envisage what sort of woman could do that to a man. She had been brought up in an openly affectionate environment, had always been honest in her relationships with men, and she couldn't imagine any woman being so devious as to use her body to flaunt a man's weakness at him.

But Alex had been badly scarred by such a woman in the past, had a distrust of giving even body attraction freely. It complicated their relationship to such an extreme that she wondered what chance their marriage would have. While she had been in America she had decided that even though they didn't have love, a warm and giving physical relationship would make them a good marriage. But although Alex might give the pleasure he had no intention of giving the warmth.

But it was done now, her word was given. And maybe in twenty years time, when she still melted bonelessly at his touch and asked nothing he didn't want to give, he would come to believe it was him and him alone that she wanted.

Morgan wasn't even out of bed the next morning when Rita Hammond burst into her bedroom unannounced. The maid had brought in her coffee a few minutes earlier, but one look at Rita Hammond's face told her she would be wiser to put the cup down out of harm's way; she was likely to get the contents tipped all over her if the hatred in the other woman's face was given full vent! She certainly didn't need to be told that Alex had told his mother they were getting married!

'So you're more devious than I would give you credit for!' the other woman attacked viciously.

Morgan swung her legs out of bed to stand up, feeling at too much of a disadvantage sitting in bed. Her white nightgown flowed silkily about her slender ankles. 'I gather you aren't pleased about the wedding?' she derided.

'Pleased! It's obvious it's only for Courtney's sake— my son has been stupid enough to take to heart the suggestion of the press that the two of you marry for the baby's sake. Well, I——'

'*Nothing* about Alex is stupid, Mrs Hammond,' she snapped. 'And I intend making a success of the marriage, no matter whose suggestion it was initially.'

'You don't love my son——'

'I *care* for him, which is just as important.' Morgan's eyes blazed. 'Alex is a fine man, I'll be proud to be his wife.'

'Over my dead body!'

Her mouth twisted. 'If necessary,' she drawled.

'I will not have you as a member of my family——'

'I'm not too thrilled about having you as one of mine,' Morgan traded insult for insult. 'But we don't have a choice when it comes to in-laws,' she snapped. 'Now if you wouldn't mind, I would like to get dressed.'

'But I do mind. I'll never accept you as my daughter-in-law, Morgan.'

'Contrary to your beliefs, Mrs Hammond, your acceptance is not important to me.' She looked coldly at the other woman. 'Not at all.'

'You'll regret this, Morgan!' the other woman almost shouted, losing her usual composure completely.

'I don't think so.'

'You'll be no happier here than Glenna was!'

'Oh, I think I will. You see, I know from the first how destructive you are. You even lie to achieve your objective.'

'You're talking about the night Alex spent in London?' Rita Hammond scorned.

'You know I am,' Morgan derided. 'I'll never fall for your lies again. Alex *was* working, and you knew damn well he was.'

'Did I?'

'Yes!' she bit out tautly.

'Did he tell you it was work?'

'Yes. And I'm more inclined to believe him than I am you.'

'Then you're a fool!'

'No, I just happen to trust the man who's going to be my husband,' Morgan said calmly.

'You're both insane!' Rita Hammond was very flushed in her anger. 'No marriage can work in these circumstances.'

'This one will,' Morgan said with certainty.

'I'll remind you that you said that when you can't take any more and leave,' the other woman scorned, going to the door.

'That will never happen,' Morgan said softly as Rita Hammond left.

The scene had been no worse than she had expected, in fact it hadn't been as bad. She had thought there might be some vitriolic comments made about Glenna at the same time, but the other woman had managed to restrain herself. No doubt pointed little barbs would continue during her married life with Alex. But she would ignore them, would ignore the woman who made them too.

'Why didn't you tell me?'

She turned with a start, very conscious of the sheerness of her nightgown, sure that Alex could see every inch of her body through the silky material. 'Tell you what?' Without undue haste she pulled on the matching négligé, knowing the two thicknesses afforded her a little more covering.

'About my mother's lying interference.' He came into her bedroom and closed the door, dressed for the office in a brown three-piece suit and cream shirt.

She shrugged, conscious of her lack of make-up, of her ruffled hair that she hadn't had a chance to brush yet. 'I didn't want to cause unnecessary friction between the two of you.'

'Unnecessary?' he echoed curtly. 'It wasn't unnecessary! My mother is positively vindictive. If she ever does anything like that again I want you to tell me immediately.'

'Yes, Alex.'

He smiled ruefully. 'And don't put on that demure act with me. After the things you just told my mother I'll never believe it.'

Morgan looked at him uncertainly. 'How much did you hear?'

'All of it,' he said grimly. 'I was on my way to say goodbye to you when I saw my mother come into your room. After your first defence of me I couldn't help listening to the rest of the conversation. You sound very sure that our marriage is going to work, Morgan,' he frowned.

'I am sure.' She moved into his arms. 'It just requires complete honesty on both sides.'

He tapped her playfully on the nose. 'And that includes telling me about any other bitchiness like this from my family. I have no doubt Janet will side with my mother, she'll probably try to stick in a few knives too.'

Morgan shook her head. 'It won't matter to me. All I want is you—and Courtney.'

His brows rose. 'In that order?'

She frowned. 'I couldn't make that choice. I already think of Courtney as my child, and you as his father. No woman should be made to choose between her child and her husband.'

Alex shook his head. 'I admired your directness from the start,' he murmured. 'But when it has to do with me I get a little nervous.'

She ran a caressing hand down his cheek, enjoying being in his arms after the stiff way they had parted last night. 'You'll get used to it.'

'I doubt it,' he retorted dryly. 'Kiss me goodbye, I have to get to work.'

She needed no further encouragement, standing on tiptoe to mould her mouth against his, kissing him with all the fervour she was capable of, feeling his lips part as she continued the assault, his arms tightening about her as he became the one doing the kissing.

'Ah, Morgan ...!' he groaned against her throat minutes later. 'You shouldn't have said no last night.'

'No,' she agreed shakily.

His lips parted hers again, demanding her full response. She still clung to him as he put her away from him, her eyes a deep smoky green, her lips swollen from his kisses. 'I'll come back for you this afternoon,' he told her briskly, pushing his tousled hair back with impatient fingers. 'Take you to the airport.'

'There's no need,' she smiled.

'I'd like to.'

'I'm beginning to realise I dislike goodbyes,' she grimaced.

'You didn't give that impression just now,' he mocked.

She shook her head. '*Public* goodbyes,' she said pointedly. 'I'd rather you met me at the airport when I come back. If you have time,' she added hastily.

'What a conscientous wife you're going to make!'

Alex gave a teasing smile. 'I'll make time. You're sure about this afternoon?'

'Very,' she nodded.

Morgan meant what she said about goodbyes, she did hate them, and although she wasn't exactly saying goodbye to her parents for ever she would be a married woman when she saw them next, would no longer be just their daughter but Alex's wife and Courtney's mother too.

She was kept very busy at the studio that first week of her return. The filming of *Power Trap* was nearing its end now for this season, everyone working flat out. She went to see her parents the following weekend, knowing that she had to actually face them with the news of her marriage to Alex.

'You don't know the man,' her father frowned. 'How can you marry him?'

'I want to,' she answered simply.

'Is it because of Court?' he demanded gruffly. 'Because I won't have you sacrificing yourself, not even for my grandson's sake.'

Morgan knew what this cost her father, how he wanted to grab at this chance to hold on to Courtney with both hands. But he held back, unsure of her reasons. 'It is partly for him,' she admitted truthfully. 'I won't deny that. But it's mainly for myself.'

'Do you love Alex?' her father growled.

'I——'

'Do you, Morgan?' her mother put in softly.

What did love mean? Wanting to be with one person. Wanting to feel his arms about you, to hold him in return. Wanting only that person's happiness, even at the expense of her own feelings. She wanted all that with Alex. Did that mean she *loved* him?

'Morgan?' her mother prompted.

She swallowed convulsively at the discovery she had

just made about herself. She didn't just want Alex physically, she wanted him in every way a woman in love could want the man of her choice. 'Yes,' she answered confidently. 'Yes, I love him.' There could be no doubting the sincerity of her words.

She loved Alex Hammond, loved him and hadn't even known that she did. This was something she just couldn't tell him; she knew his opinion of love, of its destruction.

And yet when she saw him waiting at the airport a week later she couldn't hold back her feelings, and ran into his arms, her face raised for his kiss as he caught her to him.

It had been a long week, longing to get back to him and yet having to see her contract through to the end. Her single telephone call the night before telling him of her arrival time had been very unsatisfactory, their stilted conversation telling her that they weren't only apart in miles. The softening towards her Alex had shown on that last morning had been replaced by cold suspicion; a telephone line was not the way to bridge the gulf.

But she had no restraint as she came through Customs and spotted him waiting for her; she threw herself into his arms. 'Oh, I missed you!' she groaned.

'I—Courtney's been pining for you,' he told her gruffly.

She wouldn't expect too much from him too soon. 'That's nice,' she smiled. 'Kiss me, Alex,' she encouraged throatily.

'Here?' He looked about them selfconsciously.

'Yes, here!' She looked up at him appealingly.

With a muffled groan he bent his head to kiss her, and went on kissing her, on and on, as if he never wanted to stop either.

CHAPTER SIX

At last Alex broke the contact, breathing raggedly as he looked down at her. 'Let's get out of here,' he rasped as he realised several people were openly staring at them.

Morgan put her arm through the crook of his. 'It's good to be back,' she gave him a glowing smile.

He smiled back at her, although the warmth didn't quite reach his eyes, the wariness was still in them. 'We can talk on the drive.'

She sat in the car while her luggage was loaded in the trunk of the car. 'I closed up my apartment,' she told Alex as he got in beside her. 'That's why there's so much,' she excused.

'Was it hard to leave?'

'Not at all,' she said happily as they drove through the long tunnel that took traffic in and out of Heathrow airport. How could it possibly be difficult to leave Los Angeles when she was going to be with the man she loved? She was nervous, of course she was, but she was also elated at the thought of becoming Alex's wife.

'Not even Sam?' His tone was hard.

She still felt guilty about Sam. They had become good friends the last few months, and she knew that eventually they might have drifted into a good marriage. But Joanie had been the love of Sam's life, and her death had left him devastated; Morgan could only ever have been second best to him. Her affection for Sam had been genuine, but her love for Alex was allconsuming. Saying goodbye to Sam, telling him she was actually going to marry the man who had shown her the 'agony and the ecstasy' of love had been very hard indeed, especially as she knew she was the first woman Sam had taken out seriously since his wife died.

'I can see it was,' Alex rasped. 'You must have cared for him more than you realised.'

'No, I——'

'How did your parents react to the fact that you're going to marry me?' he bit out grimly.

'They're very pleased. Alex, about Sam——'

'You owe me no explanations,' he dismissed coldly.

'Why are you so stubborn!' She was finding that loving this man didn't make her any less impatient with his cold arrogance. 'I was very fond of Sam, but I didn't love him. I'd become a—a sort of prop, after his wife died.'

Alex glanced at her. 'I didn't realise he'd been married.'

'Why should you?' she dismissed. 'I told you little or nothing about him. A lot of what I felt for him was pity, I think. He seemed so lost after Joanie died.'

This seemed to displease Alex even more, for his mouth tightened ominously. 'Your parents?' he prompted hardly.

'Were surprised. But they were very pleased when I explained to them that——' she broke off, her happiness at seeing Alex again loosening her tongue too much.

'Yes?'

'That it was the practical thing to do,' she improvised lamely.

'Practical? Yes, I suppose it is,' he nodded. 'I've arranged the wedding for Friday. I hope that meets your approval.'

Three days. Just three more days and they would be husband and wife. This time a month ago she hadn't seriously thought of marrying anyone, let alone Alex Hammond. But this time last month Glenna had still been alive.

'Yes, that—that's fine,' she agreed shakily. She had been so busy the last two weeks that she had managed to push the air crash to the back of her mind. Now it came back with a vengeance, leaving her weak and shaken.

'What is it?' Alex demanded sharply. 'Morgan? Have you changed your mind about the marriage?'

'Of course not. Have I acted as if I have?' she derided. 'No, I was just thinking about Glenna. If she hadn't died——'

'Don't think about it.' His hand came out to clasp hers. 'I'm sorry, I've been inconsiderate, questioning you like this; you must be tired. Just rest for now, we can talk later. I was going to take you out to dinner, but——'

'Oh, I'd love to go out with you,' Morgan said eagerly. 'I'll have a lie down when we get to the house and then I'll be ready to go out later, okay?'

'Only if you feel up to it.'

She was determined to. She might be marrying this man, but they had never even been out together!

'My mother is staying with Janet for a few days,' he told her as he halted the car outside the house.

Morgan smiled. 'She knew I was arriving today, hmm?'

His mouth twisted. 'I would be lying if I said anything else.'

'That's what I thought!' She walked into the house at his side, and was surprised when Symonds offered her his congratulations before having her luggage taken upstairs.

'All the staff have been informed of our marriage,' Alex told her softly. 'I thought it best.'

'Mm, especially when I move into your bedroom,' she added teasingly.

'But you won't be.'

'Alex——'

'Look, we'll discuss all this over dinner.'

'But——'

'Later, Morgan.' He kissed her firmly on the mouth to stop further speech.

After she had spent some time with Courtney Morgan did manage to fall asleep in her room for a couple of hours, although Alex's claim that she wouldn't be sharing his room disturbed her. She thought they had settled all that before she went back to the States. Well, no matter what Alex had decided in her absence, she would not settle for a sterile marriage; she wanted Courtney to eventually have brothers and sisters. It was with that thought in mind that she finally drifted off to sleep, a smile on her lips as she imagined holding Alex's baby in her arms.

She dressed with special care that evening, seeing admiration flare in Alex's eyes as she joined him in the lounge. The long green dress clung smoothly over her breasts, completely strapless, her breasts jutting out firmly beneath the clinging material, her stomach was taut and flat, her hips curving slenderly before the dress flowed softly to her ankles.

'You look beautiful!' He came forward to take her hands in his. 'I have something for you.'

'For me?' Her eyes brightened.

'Yes,' he smiled at her enthusiastic response, sliding a hand into the hip pocket of his dinner jacket, bringing out a small ring box. He flicked open the lid, revealing a delicate gold ring with a diamond and emerald setting. 'Your engagement ring. If you like it. If you don't——'

'Of course I like it!' She was still staring at the beautiful ring. 'You chose it for me, so of course I love it. It's really beautiful. Put it on for me.' She held out her hand, the nails painted the same vivid red as her lip gloss.

It was slightly loose on her finger, but not so loose it would fall off.

'I'll get it made smaller while we're on our honeymoon,' Alex promised.

'Oh, it doesn't matter——'

'Do you want to lose it?'

Considering that it looked as if it cost a fortune she certainly didn't want to do that. She shook her head. 'Okay. But it stays where it is until I have the plain gold band to take its place. It is going to be plain gold, isn't it?'

Alex chuckled as he opened the car door for her. 'When you aren't losing your temper you're quite bubbly, aren't you?' he teased.

'I don't get engaged every day of the week, Mr Hammond!'

'Believe it or not, neither do I,' he said dryly, driving the Mercedes with his usual skill.

'Have you ever been engaged before?'

'No.'

'Married?'

'No,' he derided.

'Well, Glenna never mentioned it, and I was—I was curious.' And now she knew that he hadn't actually made any commitment to the woman who had hurt him so badly. That was encouraging at least.

'Well, don't be,' he taunted. 'I've never been engaged, married, or into serious relationships for any long period of time.'

'Neither have I,' she told him lightly.

'No?' he mocked.

Morgan shot him a sharp look, not liking his tone at all. 'I refuse to argue with you tonight, Alex, not when we've just become engaged.'

'Why should you want to?'

'Because I think you just insulted me!'

'I did?'

'You know you did,' she said crossly. 'But you'll see, Alex, you're wrong about me, so very wrong.'

His eyes were glacial, his jaw rigid. 'Am I? I doubt it.' He heaved a deep sigh. 'As you said, let's not argue tonight. I hope you like the restaurant I've chosen,' he firmly changed the subject.

'I'm sure I shall!'

His mouth softened. 'Don't be angry with me, Morgan. There are thirty-eight years of cynicism and scepticism that you have to deal with.'

Her eyes flashed deeply green. 'And there are twenty-six years of independence and honesty you have to deal with!'

Alex touched her cheek gently. 'I'll cope.'

'So will I!' she vowed determinedly.

The restaurant was very full, although they were somehow shown to one of the best tables in the place, a secluded table in one corner of the room. The restaurant was styled like an old country inn, the service friendly and intimate, the lighting a soft red glow.

'I like it,' Morgan told Alex once they were seated.

'I hoped you would.' He nodded briefly to the waiter as he arrived with their champagne. 'To us,' he toasted her minutes later.

'To us,' she echoed fervently.

Alex sipped the bubbly wine, looking at her speculatively. 'That sounded very intense!'

She met his gaze steadily. 'I'm a very intense person.'

'I've noticed!'

'And I don't just mean my temper,' she glared at him.

'Let's order,' he suggested gently.

'Are you always going to shut me up by feeding me or kissing me?' she asked in a disgruntled voice.

'No,' he told her softly once the waiter had left with their order. 'Once we're married I'm going to use a much more effective method. The way I remember it, you're a silent lover—except for those deliciously spine-tingling noises you make in your throat.'

'Alex!' For all her sophistication colour flooded her cheeks, and she looked about them selfconsciously.

'Indeed, Alex,' he drawled. 'What have you done to me, Morgan McKay? I've never been known to engage in conversations like this before.'

'You were never going to be married before,' she teased, loving him so much she ached for him. 'But you said earlier that I wouldn't be sharing your bedroom when we're married,' she reminded him with a frown.

He shook his head. 'I said you wouldn't be moving into my room at the house, and you won't be. I thought we could go and look at houses tomorrow if you're feeling up to it after your flight.' He quirked dark brows questioningly.

Morgan frowned. 'Houses ...? You mean, of our own?' she gasped her surprise.

'Of course.'

'Just the three of us?'

'And a housekeeper, and possibly a maid or two. I trust you have no objection to someone else doing the cooking and cleaning while you take care of Courtney?' he mocked.

'No. But—Your mother?' she frowned.

'Doesn't like the idea at all,' he confirmed dryly.

'Then why——'

'I'm not marrying to please my mother, Morgan. Far from it!' he rasped, revealing more than words the pressure he had been under during her week of absence to change his mind about marrying her. 'But I remember the problems you said you had facing you, and buying our own house would solve two of them—

seeing too much of my mother and living in the same house as her. You've chosen for us all to remain in England, so obviously you feel you can cope with that. The last problem I am unable to do anything about,' he finished harshly.

That they didn't love each other! No, they didn't, but she loved him, and she was going to do her damnedest to make him fall in love with her. 'Tell me some more about the houses,' she encouraged huskily.

He gave her a searching look. 'You like the idea,' he said at last.

'I love it!' she smiled. 'Although not too far from your mother, so that she can visit Courtney whenever she wants to.'

'After the way she's treated you that's very generous of you,' he said stiffly.

'She's his grandmother,' she explained simply.

They had an enjoyable meal together, in fact it was a long time since Morgan could remember enjoying herself like this. Perhaps she never had; she had never been in love before.

'Nightcap?' Alex queried huskily when they got back to the house, a silent house where the servants had already gone to bed.

She was very conscious of the fact that there was no malignant presence of Rita Hammond upstairs tonight just waiting for their ascent, and that fact alone made her feel almost lightheaded. Or perhaps it was the champagne doing that? She didn't care what it was, she loved the feeling. 'I'd love one.' She followed him into the lounge, where a fire had been left burning for their return, as the September evenings were very cool.

'Brandy?'

'Fine,' she nodded. 'I had a lovely time tonight, Alex.'

'So did I.' The admission seemed somehow to be

forced from him. 'We'll have to do it often when we're married. I trust you'll have no objection to leaving Courtney with a reliable housekeeper on the occasional evening?'

'Not at all,' she smiled. 'After all, I'll be your wife too, not just Courtney's mother.' She became suddenly serious. 'Will we adopt him as our own, Alex?'

He handed her her brandy, sitting down beside her on the sofa. 'I thought we might.'

She nodded. 'I think that when he's older, and we tell him the truth about his parents, knowing we cared enough to make him legally ours will make him feel more wanted and not as if he's ever been a burden to us. Especially when he has brothers and sisters to contend with.' She gave Alex a sideways glance, waiting for his reaction.

'Brothers *and* sisters?' he repeated slowly.

'Oh yes, I've always wanted a family. Both Glenna and I——' she broke off, her face suddenly blanching.

'It's all right, Morgan.' Alex's arm came about her shoulders as he held her close to him. 'I still feel the pain of losing them too.'

She buried her face in his chest. 'I'm sorry, I didn't mean to spoil the evening.'

'You haven't.' He took the glass of brandy out of her shaking hand and put it beside his on the coffee table, tilting her chin to wipe away her tears with his thumbtips. 'You're a warm and loving woman who cares deeply for people.' He kissed her gently on the lips. 'I think a family sounds a wonderful idea. After all, I have the best part,' he mocked.

'You think so?' she teased him.

'I know so.' He moulded her body against his. 'We have the house to ourselves, Morgan,' he prompted softly.

She stiffened, sobering completely, the effects of the

champagne a thing of the past. 'We don't really.' She moved away from him with a light laugh. 'Symonds and the other servants are in the house, aren't they?'

He nodded. 'In their own quarters.'

'We'll be married in three days, Alex,' she dismissed. 'Besides, I'm tired tonight.'

His mouth twisted sardonically, and he moved to pour himself another glass of brandy. 'You're using that excuse before we're married,' he taunted. 'What comes afterwards, the headache?'

'I think you're being insulting——'

'Believe it,' he bit out grimly, staring sightlessly at the fire. 'I've already told you, I will not be controlled by the physical attraction I feel for you.'

'I'm not——'

'Go to bed, Morgan,' he ordered roughly. 'You said you were tired, so go.'

'Alex——'

'Go!'

'What are you going to do?' she asked anxiously.

'Finish my drink and go to my own bed, of course,' he derided.

She paused at the door. 'Will we still go and look at houses tomorrow?'

He nodded distantly. 'If you wish.'

'I do. Alex . . .?'

He didn't even turn. 'Yes?'

She sighed. 'I wish I could explain—You'll soon understand the reason for my reluctance now.' There was pleading in her voice.

'I understand it already,' he scorned. 'The longer you keep a man waiting for your body the more he's going to want you. Woman's logic!'

'Not at all, Alex.' She could see there was no talking to him tonight, especially when she didn't intend telling him the whole truth. Not yet. 'I'll see you in the morning.'

'No doubt,' he bit out tautly.

Morgan made her way slowly up to her bedroom. She hadn't wanted to deny Alex tonight, in fact it would have been all too easy to say yes to him. But it was very important to her, for Alex's sake as well as her own, that they wait until after they were married. Her wedding gift to him was priceless, beyond compare, all the more so to Alex because of his bitterness and distrust of woman. She *would* give him the gift of herself gladly on their wedding night. And then let him dare to accuse her of being promiscuous!

It was so very easy choosing a house the next day. Alex had wonderful taste, and most of his likes and dislikes seemed to coincide with hers, so that the choosing of the six-bedroomed Regency-style house was a mutual one.

Morgan liked the house because it was more in the country than the Hammond one, had room for a stable and a couple of horses on the land attached. Riding had been something she had enjoyed as a child but had little opportunity to do since then. The garden was big, but not too big, something she would like to keep tidy herself, with help from Courtney as he got older, no doubt. And it had a small family pool out the back of it too.

'I'll teach Courtney to swim,' she said excitedly as they drove home after dealing with the legal formalities of buying a house in England.

Alex had been very cold towards her when they had first met this morning, but as the day progressed he had seemed to thaw, throwing her an indulgent smile now. 'He can't even focus yet,' he taunted. 'Give him a chance. And with all these activities you intend to become involved in—gardening, riding, taking care of Courtney, teaching him to swim—how do you think you're going to find time to resume your career.'

'I'll wait until he goes to school,' she shrugged.

'You could be a thing of the past by then,' he warned softly. 'The public are very fickle, they forget so easily.'

'I could have other children to think about by then anyway,' she said abruptly.

'I'm not trying to push you back out to work, Morgan,' he said with amusement. 'I'm as chauvinistic as the next man, and I don't relish the thought of my wife going out to work. And in normal circumstances I would probably ask you not to do so. But these aren't normal circumstances, you're marrying me because of Courtney, because of a sense of duty to him.'

'And because I wanted you,' she reminded him with challenge.

His mouth twisted. 'You'll have to forgive me if I feel a little sceptical about that,' he taunted. 'There hasn't been much evidence of it lately. Most women seem to find the idea of a physical relationship interesting until they have a ring on their finger, then sex just becomes bargaining power.'

'You're very cynical,' she sighed.

'I've learnt to be,' he nodded grimly. 'Most men do in time.'

Morgan couldn't fight this cynicism now, knew that she wouldn't be able to until they were married and she could show him how wrong he was about her.

Rita Hammond came back to the house on the morning of the wedding, claiming haughtily that if Alex insisted on going through with this ridiculous marriage the least she could do was give him her moral support.

Morgan had to smile at the last. Alex didn't need anyone's support, least of all that of his mother!

'White?' Janet Fairchild came into Morgan's bedroom as she was getting dressed for the wedding.

Morgan bristled angrily at the other woman's ridicule of the colour of her wedding dress. 'Some of us are entitled to wear the colour,' she replied haughtily.

'I know,' Janet nodded. 'I was.'

'And so am I.' Morgan straightened the soft chiffon dress about her hips, a tiny white lace cap attached to her flaming hair.

'I doubt it,' Janet drawled. 'I must say I'm surprised at Alex's stupidity at marrying you. I'd always credited him with more sense. And why on earth you have to move into your own house I have no idea. This house is big enough for ten families!'

Morgan looked at the other woman with hard green eyes. 'Alex and I do not intend making the same mistakes Glenna and Mark did. Why did you never move in here with your husband?' she taunted.

'Because Mother would eat Charles alive,' Janet said bluntly.

Morgan's mouth twisted. 'I doubt she would ever have the same effect on me, nevertheless I can do without her vitriolic comments day and night.'

'Are you and Alex lovers?'

'None of your damned business!' Morgan told her in a controlled voice.

Blue eyes hardened. 'I've seen the way he watches you.' Janet shrugged. 'It would also be a way of explaining this madness.'

'Alex doesn't consider it madness,' Morgan snapped.

'I don't suppose you do either,' Janet sneered. 'A career as an actress, when all you have is your body and your beauty, can't last very long. Marriage to a rich man means you can't lose. If the marriage lasts you live in luxury, if it fails you get a nice healthy settlement. You're as clever as Glenna, Morgan, maybe more so.'

Morgan's hand seemed to move of its own volition, moving in a slow arc to make hard contact with Janet Fairchild's cheek. The other woman gasped, her own hand going up to the reddening area, as she stared at Morgan in disbelief.

The eyes hardened to hatred, her mouth twisted viciously. 'You'll regret that, Morgan!' she spat out the words.

'I don't think so.' Morgan was shaking with the reaction of losing her temper so completely, but she refused to let Janet Fairchild see that. She would allow no insults to Glenna on *her* wedding day!

'Oh, but you will.' Her hand dropped to her side, the mark of Morgan's fingers clearly visible on her cheek. 'I'll make sure of it!' She turned on her heel and slammed out of the room.

Morgan could no longer control the shaking; she dropped down on to the bed, breathing deeply. If she didn't love Alex so desperately this constant and vicious hatred from his family would have her running far away from here, Courtney or no Courtney. She knew she had made even more of an enemy of Janet Fairchild today, and that the other woman would need careful watching.

But there was no evidence of the other woman's antagonism as they drove to the wedding, in fact her pleasantly charming manner was more unsettling than the open hatred she had displayed earlier when they were alone.

Alex looked magnificent in a deep blue suit and snowy white shirt, his gaze admiring as he looked at Morgan in her knee-length white dress, her bouquet made up of pure white roses.

There were few guests at the actual wedding, although the reception being held at the house was a different matter. Rita Hammond considered it her duty to have all the relatives and family friends at her eldest son's wedding reception, even if she didn't approve of his choice of bride.

'Formidable, aren't they?' Alex mocked against Morgan's earlobe as the last guest had been welcomed and the two of them could relax a little.

'A little,' she agreed dryly, wondering at the family's reaction to a second gathering like this within the space of a month, for two such different occasions. Most of them looked a little dazed by it all!

'We'll leave as soon as we can,' he promised softly.

They were spending their first night together as husband and wife in London, taking a plane to the States tomorrow, staying overnight with her parents before flying to Barbados for their three-week honeymoon. Morgan could hardly wait for the time they could be alone.

'I'd like that,' she acknowledged.

'The house will be ready to move into by the time we get back.'

They had spent a frantic two days choosing fabrics and colour schemes so that the house could be furnished and decorated for their return, Courtney's room had given Morgan the most pleasure; it was in the predictable Disney characters, of course. The fact that it was all going to be ready when they got back meant she wouldn't have to move in with this den of lions again.

As if reading some of her thoughts, Alex asked, 'What happened with Janet earlier?' His tone had hardened perceptively. 'She came out of your room looking as if someone had hit her.'

'*I* had,' Morgan admitted simply. 'She was insulting, and so I hit her.' She looked at him in challenge.

'Didn't you know that wives are supposed to let husbands protect them?' he taunted, not in the least concerned that she had struck his sister.

She smiled her relief, not at all sure what his reaction had been going to be. 'You weren't my husband then.'

'But I am now,' he reminded her huskily. 'So any more—insults, tell me and I'll deal with them, in my own way,' he added grimly.

She had no doubt he would too. Always an independent woman, she found it strange to think that she now had someone to rely on, someone who would help her fight her battles. But it was a two-way thing; she would help Alex in any way she could too.

By the time they left just after eight o'clock she had a throbbing headache. She had met so many relatives of Alex's it made her head spin; she had fenced barbs with Rita Hammond in so many two-edged conversations she could no longer think straight, and all the time she had been conscious of Janet Fairchild's derisive glance, as if she knew something Morgan didn't but wasn't yet prepared to divulge it. Saying goodbye to Courtney made it all the worse, and the thought of three weeks without him seemed like a lifetime.

But she daren't even mention the headache to Alex, remembering all too vividly his taunt about her developing headaches after they were married to avoid sharing his bed.

'Tired?' he asked as she leant her head back weakly against the car seat.

'A little,' she admitted.

His hand came out to grasp hers. 'We can eat in our suite if you would prefer that.'

Eat? heavens, the thought of food nauseated her! 'I—Fine,' she agreed weakly, closing her eyes and pretending to be asleep.

When the sleep became a reality she had no idea, but suddenly Alex was shaking her gently to wake her up. 'We're at the hotel,' he told her softly. 'Feeling better? Headache gone?' he prompted huskily.

Morgan sat up, her eyes widened. 'You knew?'

'You're very pale, and your eyes seemed sensitive to the light. Of course I knew,' he rasped, straightening in his seat. 'Don't be afraid of me, Morgan,' he warned.

'I'm not,' she snapped. 'I just didn't want any more accusations like the ones of the other evening. The headache has gone now, anyway,' she told him abruptly.

He touched her cheek gently. 'The other evening I was suffering from that most common of male ailments—sexual frustration,' he taunted. 'If you have a headache then perhaps you would like an early night—alone?'

His thoughtfulness, after the tension of the day, made her eyes swim with tears. 'The headache really has gone, Alex,' she choked.

'Do I take that to mean you would rather *not* have an early night alone?' he teased.

She smiled. 'I have no objection to the early night, but definitely not alone.'

He laughed softly, getting out of the car as the doorman of the hotel came over to open Morgan's door for her. 'We'll discuss that after dinner,' he promised.

The hotel was one of the most luxurious in London, and the honeymoon suite had been reserved for them. Morgan's eyes widened as she heard this. She would have thought Alex the sort of man to prefer to keep quiet about their newly married state, not broadcast it so obviously. Although it might have been a little difficult to keep it quiet anyway, as they were both covered in confetti!

Alex had the arrogance and bearing to have the best service wherever he went, and within five minutes of entering the hotel they and their luggage had been effortlessly transported to the top floor, their luxurious suite occupying most of it.

Dinner was a lighthearted affair. Morgan was not even aware of what she was eating, enjoying Alex's company too much to really care.

'Now about that early night . . .?' He raised dark brows as they sat together in the lounge. The hotel was so tall that none of the noise of London could be heard all the way up here, giving a strangely disorientated feeling.

'It's after eleven!' she taunted.

'In London that's early.'

She smiled. 'I'd like to shower first.'

'Of course. I'll use the other bathroom,' he nodded distantly.

Alex's abrupt attitude made her wonder if he weren't a little disconcerted by their wedding night too. That thought gave her a little more confidence in herself and the night ahead of them.

She took her time in the bathroom, and her whole body felt smoothly oiled and perfumed by the time she had finished, smelling of her favourite Estée Lauder body lotion. The sheer white nightgown did nothing to hide the perfection of her slender curves, being almost completely transparent, reaching down to her bare feet.

For a moment when she entered the lounge she thought Alex was still in the second bathroom, then she saw a movement by the window, walking over to his side to gaze over the thousands of glittering lights that were London.

He turned to look at her as he sensed her presence, his breath catching in his throat as the perfection of her body was clearly revealed to him. Morgan looked up at him with fearless green eyes—his bare chest darkly tanned, covered in thick dark hair, his shoulders powerfully muscled, black silk pyjama trousers, his only clothing, resting low down on his hips. He looked magnificent, his eyes becoming smoky grey with desire.

'Morgan . . .?' he groaned.

She moistened her lips with the tip of her tongue, not wanting to talk, but knowing there were some things she had to tell him before they made love. 'Have you noticed that I've worn white today, Alex?' she asked gruffly.

His eyes narrowed. 'I've noticed,' he nodded.

'I—I've worn it for a reason.'

'Yes?' he said tautly.

She launched into speech before she lost her nerve, his cynicism making it hard for her to talk at all. 'When Glenna and I were children, we used to talk a lot about when we got married. Of course it was all a fantasy,' she laughed at the idealist she had been then. 'By the time we'd grown up there were no dashing heroes about like Errol Flynn. But it was fun to dream anyway. And we made each other a promise, one that we both kept.'

'Yes?' Alex was very tense.

She looked at him with unblinking green eyes. 'Alex, do you mind having a virgin for a bride?' she asked bluntly.

His eyes narrowed, his arms tightening on her arms, hurting her. 'A virgin?' he echoed disbelievingly.

'I'm afraid so,' she nodded. 'And you don't find many of them at twenty-six any more!'

'Don't joke about this, Morgan,' he rasped, shaking her slightly. 'It's too serious. Are you telling me the truth?'

'A fun-loving actress with no morals?' she mocked brittly. 'I'm afraid so, Alex.'

He released her, drawing in a harsh breath, then expelling it slowly, looking at her as if he had never seen her before. 'Is this the reason you held back the other night?'

She nodded. 'A shock, isn't it?' She hated herself for making light about something that was so important to her, but Alex's feelings, other than surprise, weren't yet apparent to her. 'In this day and age too! But I'm afraid I've always considered my body, and myself, to be more important than becoming just another notch on some man's bedpost. I suppose I could have started collecting notches myself, but somehow that never appealed to me either. It's too easy to fall into a sexual relationship with someone now, and I've never liked doing the easy things in life. Of course, if the idea of being the man to initiate me into making love doesn't appeal to you ...' She looked at him challengingly, holding her breath as she waited for his answer.

'You know it does,' Alex finally spoke. 'You're one hell of a woman, Morgan Hammond,' he shook his head. 'I'm beginning to wonder just what I've taken on by marrying you. A virgin, and yet you married me partly because you wanted me!' he realised incredulously.

'Terrible, isn't it?' she mocked, relief flooding through her. Alex did still want her! 'You make me feel quite shameless, Mr Hammond.'

'I'll tell you how I feel as I make love to you,' he groaned against her throat. 'And I'll try not to hurt you. Dear God, Morgan, you aren't innocent enough not to have——'

'No, no, I've taken care of that,' she assured him hastily. 'As you say, I'm not that innocent.'

'Thank God—I wouldn't want anything to spoil your pleasure.'

'Alex——!'

He looked down at her with amused eyes. 'I think you make me feel shameless too,' he smiled, swinging her up into his arms with ease.

Her arms encircled his throat. 'What are you doing?' She snuggled against him.

'Whatever it is, you aren't fighting it,' he derided, striding determinedly towards the bedroom they were to share tonight.

'I trust you implicitly,' she murmured against his throat, her lips warm and probing.

He seemed to tense. 'Implicitly?'

She looked up at him. 'Yes. Now tell me why you carried me here?' she asked dreamily as he put her down on the double bed. 'I would quite happily have walked.'

'It was the nearest I could come to carrying you over the threshold,' he told her throatily as he came down on the bed beside her. 'Morgan, are you sure you want me to be the first——'

Her fingertips over his lips stopped further words. 'I'm very sure. I want you, remember? You're the only man I've ever wanted.'

'Wanton hussy!'

She squirmed with pleasure as his mouth plundered hers, tasting and devouring as the first passion overtook him, his powerful thighs surging against hers. She kissed him back wildly, aware that the situation was spiralling quickly out of Alex's control, a control he had sworn never to lose.

'Morgan!' he buried his face in her throat, soothing the passion between them to simmering point with his slow caresses down the length of her body. 'Darling——!' His mouth claimed hers gently this time, his lips moving erotically against hers, his hand travelling from her hip to capture one thrusting breast through the silky material of her nightgown, moving with slow caressing movements over the taut peak, the caress causing a pleasurable sensation down her spine.

One thin shoulder-strap was slipped down her

shoulder, and her breast was bared to the warm cavern of his mouth, his tongue tasting and sucking the nipple further into the hot vortex, making Morgan cry out with pleasure, hardly aware that the silky gown had been slipped completely from her body. Alex slid down her body with it as his hands continued to caress her breasts, and fire shot through her as he kissed her inner thigh with nibbling caresses.

'Alex——!' she groaned as a sensation such as she had never known before surged through her body, her arms and legs thrashing about beneath him.

'Don't fight it, darling,' he encouraged huskily, his face flushed with his own arousal. 'This is all part of making love.'

'But I—I can't—Oh!' she moaned as the pleasure became too much for her. 'Alex, am I——'

'Not yet,' his mouth returned to hers. 'You aren't ready yet. I forget how inexperienced you are. You drive me insane with wanting you, Morgan,' he groaned in an aching voice.

'Show me how to please you, what you like,' she encouraged eagerly.

His mouth twisted. 'I don't know what I like from you yet.' He lay back on the bed. 'You'll just have to find out for yourself, won't you?' He looked at her encouragingly.

He liked everything, it seemed—every touch, every caress, the way she kissed his hardened thighs as she slipped the pyjama trousers off his body; both of them were completely naked now, even the sight of her nakedness lovingly bent over him causing him to shudder with pleasure.

'I think I like it too much!' he groaned, stopping her caresses. 'No more, Morgan. I can't take it!'

It was her turn to be caressed once again, his touch raising her to such ecstasy that when his body at last joined with hers she cried out only once at the moment of penetration, her movements matching his as if by instinct after that, their bodies reaching a tumultuous climax in unison, the moment held and captured only for a moment before it spiralled out of reach, leaving them spent and exhausted in each other's arms.

CHAPTER SEVEN

MORGAN woke with a feeling of well-being she had never known before, her body having a languorous ache that made it throb and glow at one and the same time, the body that Alex had claimed as his once more in the night, her own claim being made just as strongly. It had happened so easily, so naturally. Both of them had seemed to wake at the same time, turning to each other compulsively, making love slowly this time, with none of the driving fierceness that had claimed them last night. And yet the result had been the same, that bone-melting pleasure that actually made it seem as if they became one being, feeling the same pleasure, the same ecstasy. Morgan had known too much of the uncertainty of loving Alex, now she knew the ecstasy once again. There was no doubt which emotion she preferred!

'What are you smiling about?' Alex asked lazily beside her.

She turned comfortably in his arms, her head resting on his shoulder. 'I was thinking of you.'

He smiled. 'I like the idea of that. Erotic thoughts, were they?' he teased.

'Definitely!' she laughed, loving this new relaxed Alex even more than the old one.

'Feel like putting those thoughts into action?' he encouraged throatily.

She moved above him, pinning him to the matress with her light weight. 'I was thinking,' she said slowly, suggestively, 'that I would overpower you with the sight of my naked body on yours, that I would kiss and caress you all over. Then I thought—Alex, what are you doing?' she squealed as his hands closed possessively about her hips.

'Putting words into action,' he growled. 'You've aroused me just by talking about making love to you.'

'But I didn't. *I* was going to make love to *you*.'

'Be my guest.' He lay back invitingly. 'Or my wanton wife. I think I prefer the latter,' he smiled roguishly.

If the waiter who brought their breakfast noticed the silly smiles on their faces then he gave no indication of it, but served their meal with straight-faced efficiency before leaving them to it.

Morgan spluttered with laughter once they were alone, unable to contain her humour any longer as Alex tried his best to look his usual dignified self, dressed casually in a cream shirt and brown trousers as they sat at the dining-room table, Morgan just as casually dressed in white trousers and a white blouse.

He scowled at her laughter. 'I wish I hadn't chosen the damned honeymoon suite! It broadcasts the fact that we've been making love all night.'

'And couldn't we be doing that in one of the other suites too?' she teased.

'Of course. But——'

'Oh, Alex, I don't give a damn if the whole world knows!' Morgan stood up to go round the table, putting her arms around his neck and over his chest, resting her head on the top of his.

'They will if you walk around glowing like that all day,' he muttered.

'You put the glow there!' She refused to be daunted.

He stood up abruptly, turning to capture her hand in his, marching her into the bedroom.

'Alex, I'm hungry——'

'So am I. And maybe even later we might eat,' he growled moodily.

In the end they didn't bother with breakfast at all, but ordered an early lunch. The same waiter served the meal, his eyebrows rising slightly at the cold food put outside from breakfast. This time Alex laughed too once the boy had left.

Morgan stretched languorously. 'Do you suppose all honeymoons are like this?'

He smiled at her indulgently, the same satiation that was in her face reflected in his eyes. 'I don't give a damn about other honeymoons, ours is—beautiful.'

'Yes,' she returned his smile. 'I'm glad I married you, Alex.'

'So am I,' he laughed. 'Now eat your lunch, we have a plane to catch.'

Even the long plane journey to Los Angeles couldn't dim her happiness; she seemed to find an endless stream of subjects to talk to Alex about, although the times they sat in silence were equally enjoyable.

She was more in love than ever, tied to Alex by invisible threads, and although she knew he didn't return her love, he did enjoy their lovemaking as much as she did.

They hired a car once they got to Los Angeles airport, Morgan having sold her car before leaving for England this time, as she had sold everything else she no longer needed.

'Do you think you'll miss it?' Alex glanced at her as they began the drive to her parents' home, seeming as much at home driving on the right-hand side of the road as he did on the left.

'Los Angeles?' She shrugged. 'It's been my home for the last two years, of course I'll miss it. But I won't pine for it.' She put her hand on his thigh. 'I have something much better now.'

'I'm glad you didn't say you wouldn't miss it at all,' he frowned. 'Because you're sure to.'

'But not so much that it will matter, you'll see,' she said with certainty.

'I hope so.' The frown still creased his brow.

Morgan smiled mockingly. 'You've made me well and truly yours now, Alex, it's a little late for you to start having doubts.' She slanted him a mischievous look. 'We could always stop at a motel and I'll do my best to allay these sudden doubts of yours.'

His mouth quirked. 'I think I might be able to wait until tonight—with a lot of restraint,' he drawled.

Her hand tightened on his thigh, feeling his instantaneous response. 'It already is night in England.'

'Witch!'

She removed her hand. 'But if you would rather wait . . .'

'I don't *want* to,' he moved restlessly, 'but I'm going to.' He gave her a teasing glance. 'Mainly because I know it will be as much agony for you as it will be for me!'

She had held back none of her response to him, not the night before, and certainly not today. She had revelled in their lovemaking, felt no inhibitions in anything Alex said or did to her, at anything he showed her to do to him. It had all been making love, and in that they were completely compatible.

She smiled with a secret knowledge. 'My parents always go to bed early,' she explained at his questioning look.

'Meaning we'll be able to too?'

'Meaning we'd better!'

He laughed huskily. 'Maybe we should have saved this visit until the end of our honeymoon; I can hardly keep my hands off you!'

'Meaning you think you'll be able to in three weeks' time?' She gave him a scandalised look.

'Meaning you'll probably have become a little more elusive by then,' he said hardly.

She didn't argue with him, knowing that this was

another of those times when only her actions could prove her innocence, and three weeks of Alex's lovemaking certainly wouldn't be enough to satisfy her. She wanted a lifetime.

Her parents greeted her warmly, Alex reservedly; they had only met him once at the wedding before the air crash. But Alex was his most charming, and her own happiness in their marriage couldn't be doubted, so much so that by the time they all retired for bed that evening even her father had thawed towards Alex.

'Courtney is very important to him.' Alex spoke softly as he undressed for bed.

'Yes.' Morgan sat on the side of the bed unashamedly watching him. She enjoyed the nakedness of his body, knew every hard-muscled inch of it intimately.

'When Courtney is a little older we'll bring him over to see your parents.'

'Mom said it may not be too long before Dad's well enough to fly.'

Alex nodded, peeling the shirt from his body, his muscles rippling powerfully. 'Maybe they can come over for the christening.'

'Maybe.' The conversation ceased to be important as Alex took off the rest of his clothes and stood naked in front of her, unashamedly virile. 'Alex . . .!'

'Mm?' he looked at her with questioning eyes, darkening to black at the hunger in her green depths. 'How do you do it?' he murmured as he came towards her. 'How do you manage to arouse me with just a look?'

'I do?' She stood up as he slowly stripped the clothes from her body.

'You do,' he acknowledged grimly.

She began to caress him, slowly erasing that grimness from his face, putting desire and passion there in its place, until finally he could remain apart from her no longer.

'Have there been a lot of women, Alex?' she asked later, their passion spent for the moment, her head resting on his shoulder as she idly caressed the dark hair curling on his chest.

His arms tightened. 'What sort of question is that to ask a new husband?' he growled.

'An honest one.' She looked up at him. 'One that requires an answer.'

His mouth was taut. 'I have no intention of discussing such a subject on my honeymoon.'

'Why not?' She leant on her elbow looking down at him. 'You can't deny that you're a fantastic lover.'

'Morgan——'

'Oh, I know, your English reserve means that you don't talk about such things,' she teased in the face of the dark cloud gathering over his eyes. 'But speaking for myself, I think you make love beautifully.'

'You have nothing to compare it with!' he rasped.

She frowned down at him. 'I know the difference between drowning in pleasure and lying here like a stone.'

'Morgan, I'm sorry,' his voice softened at her hurt tone. 'Of course you know, just as I do. And there have been quite a few women,' he answered her question. 'Although I've learnt to be more discriminating in recent years.'

'Your family doesn't seem to think so!'

'Damn my family!' Anger flared in his dark grey eyes. 'You aren't married to them.'

'Thank God!' she shuddered.

'I didn't come all this way to discuss my family,' he scowled. 'Can't you think of something more interesting to do?'

'Oh yes,' she laughed happily, at once drowning in his possession.

She surveyed the bruises on her body the next morning with a smile of deep satiation. Alex's second lovemaking of last night had been far from gentle, and if anything it had been better than ever before.

He stirred in the bed beside her, opening sleepy eyes, becoming fully alert as he saw she was already awake. His brows lowered over angry grey eyes as he too saw the bruises, and he touched them gently. 'Did I do that?' he groaned in disbelief.

'Mm,' she confirmed lightly.

'God, I'm an animal!' he said in disgust. 'I must have hurt you.'

'No. And look,' Morgan touched his shoulder with soft fingertips.

He looked down at the ragged flesh her nails had raked during a moment of exquisite ecstasy, grinning widely. 'I wonder if we'll both survive the honeymoon!'

Survive it they did! It was a time of lazing on the beach, of preparing and eating leisurely meals together, but most of all a time of discovering each other, of a single caress igniting a flame that often took hours to quench.

Alex had hired a villa, and apart from the girl who came in to clean every morning they saw no one. Their beach was a private one, and on the last day Morgan finally persuaded her husband to bathe naked, something he had been reluctant to do.

'We could get arrested for this,' he told her as they walked hand in hand into the blue water.

She gave him a teasing look. 'This is nothing to what we'll be doing on the beach later!'

Alex laughed throatily. He had laughed a lot during their three weeks alone together, and was nothing like the cold austere man who had gone to Los Angeles to see her that first time. She hoped he would never return.

But the closer they got to England the next day the more withdrawn and terse Alex became, despite her efforts to tease him out of it. By the time they began the drive back from Heathrow to pick up Courtney it was almost imposible to believe the man at her side had made love to her on the beach in broad daylight the day before, that he had chased her back across the golden sand to the villa wearing nothing but his wedding ring.

Barbados seemed a lifetime away, not a day, and Morgan was feeling thoroughly miserable about the change in her husband by the time they reached the Hammond house.

'We won't be staying, will we, Alex?' she prompted anxiously. Her mother-in-law's probing taunts weren't something she welcomed right now. She was having a hard enough time reconciling herself to the fact that Alex had returned to his unapproachable self without that!

He glanced at his watch as they walked towards the house. 'It's twelve-thirty, almost time for lunch,' he told her pointedly.

'But——'

'We can hardly grab Courtney and run,' he derided. 'Don't be such a child, Morgan!'

Dull colour flooded her cheeks. She had completely lost her own protective shield during their honeymoon, had become used to Alex's words of admiration and encouragement rather than his aloofness. Her mask of sophistication slipped easily back into place as she watched Rita Hammond greet her son warmly before giving a cool nod in her direction.

'Did you have a nice holiday in Barbados, darling?' Rita Hammond asked Alex as they went through to the lounge, Morgan trailing along behind them.

'Barbados is always—pleasant,' he drawled in reply,

stretching his long length in one of the comfortable armchairs.

Morgan gave him a sharp look. Pleasant? Their honeymoon had been *pleasant*! Her expression was cool as she sensed Rita Hammond's triumphant gaze on her, meeting the blue-eyed gaze challengingly. 'If you'll both excuse me I think I'll go and see Courtney,' she said stiltedly, not waiting for either of them to answer her but sweeping out of the room.

She didn't stop until she stood outside Courtney's room, taking time to steady her breathing, feeling the familiar tension at being anywhere near Rita Hammond.

Alex's sudden coldness after the warmth of the last three weeks cut into her like a knife. She hadn't believed it was possible after the degree of intimacy they had attained, when only a look or a smile was needed to tell them what the other desired. A shield had fallen over Alex's inner emotions now, leaving only the cynical stranger she had known before.

And she wouldn't let him do that to them! Soon they would be at their own home, alone together again except for the baby. Whatever was bothering Alex she meant to find out as soon as possible; there would be no festering misunderstandings in this marriage if she could help it; they had too much to lose now.

But it seemed Alex had other ideas than their going home to be alone!

'I'll drop you and Courtney off at the house,' he told her over lunch. 'I have to go into the office for a couple of hours this afternoon.'

Morgan blinked her surprise; he hadn't mentioned anything about this on the drive here. 'Do you have to?' she asked stiffly, very conscious of his mother's avid attention on their conversation.

His mouth tightened. 'I would hardly be going if I didn't have to,' he snapped. 'I've been away for over three weeks already—Hammond Industries doesn't run itself, you know.'

She flinched at the way he made it seem as if he wished he hadn't spent the three weeks honeymooning with her, as if it had been time he had wasted. 'I do know,' she replied coldly, holding back the tremor from her voice. How could he talk to her like this in front of his mother?

'It would seem the honeymoon is over,' Rita Hammond drawled with satisfaction.

Alex's hard gaze flickered briefly over Morgan. 'It would seem so,' he agreed tautly.

'The newspapers got hold of the story of your wedding, by the way,' his mother told him. 'The press have been most intrusive.'

'We know,' Alex acknowledged abruptly.

It had been the one upset to their honeymoon. They had left the villa to go into the nearest small town to pick up fresh supplies, and Alex had been instantly cornered by a member of the press also on holiday there, wanting an exclusive about their marriage. Alex's reply had been far from polite!

'Is Courtney ready, Morgan?' he asked tersely now. 'I think we should be going.'

'But your coffee——'

'I don't want any,' Alex cut across his mother's objection. 'Morgan?'

The query seemed to come as an afterthought, and Morgan felt the pain in her heart deepen. How different this meal had been from the ones they had been preparing for themselves at the villa; their happiness together then had been unmistakable. Alex couldn't seem to wait to get rid of her for a few hours now! 'No, thank you,' she refused abruptly, standing up. 'I'll go and get Courtney—Mrs Ford said she would have him ready to leave after lunch.'

Courtney was indeed ready to leave, his clothes

were in a suitcase, his nursery things all packed into boxes, while the baby himself was fast asleep.

'I shall miss him,' Mrs Ford said ruefully as she handed the shawl-wrapped baby to Morgan.

'Please feel free to come and visit him any time you want to,' Morgan invited warmly. 'You'll always be welcome.'

'Thank you, I'd like that,' the other woman accepted shyly.

Morgan waited in the lounge with Rita Hammond while Alex and Symonds loaded the car up with Courtney's things; the silence between the two women was filled with tension—on Morgan's part at least, Rita Hammond looked as confident as ever. And why shouldn't she when her son had just told her his honeymoon had been *pleasant*! The description still rankled.

'So you failed to keep my son's attention even for the honeymoon,' Rita scorned. 'I knew it, of course. You're the same butterfly as Glenna.'

'Leave Glenna out of this!' Morgan ground out.

'Gladly,' the other woman dismissed haughtily. 'And I'll leave you out of it too once Alex realises the full extent of his mistake in marrying you. It's obvious he's already regretting his impetuosity!'

The baby stirred restlessly in her arms, as if even in his sleep he could sense the antagonism about him. Morgan gave up any idea of this conversation with Rita Hammond turning out to be a pleasant one, and left the house with her head held high. Alex and Symonds were just putting the last of the boxes in the car as she came down the steps, and Alex came forward to help her, handing her into the back of the car.

'Perhaps you could go and thank your mother for lunch,' she told Alex stiffly. 'I'm afraid I forgot.'

He gave her a probing glance before turning to go

back into the house. His mother was at his side when he returned.

'Could I hold Courtney for a few minutes—please?' she added as an imperious afterthought.

Morgan handed him to the other woman, seeing how the harsh features relaxed into a smile as she gazed down at her grandson. Maybe there was hope for the other woman yet, if she could feel love for the baby! 'Come and see him any time you would like to,' she said impulsively.

Cold blue eyes raked over her disdainfully. 'I intended to,' Rita told Morgan indignantly. 'He is my grandson.'

'And it's Morgan's home,' Alex put in softly, taking Courtney to put him back into Morgan's arms. She gave him a grateful smile for his defence of her.

'And my son's!'

He shrugged. 'Morgan will spend more time there than I shall.'

'Thank you,' Morgan told him quietly as they drove the ten miles to their own house.

'It's the truth,' he dismissed tersely. 'And as the two of you don't get along . . .'

She chewed on her bottom lip, braving the hardness of his profile. 'Alex, did you really think our honeymoon was only pleasant?' Her mouth twisted as she asked.

He didn't even glance at her. 'I believe I said Barbados was pleasant, I didn't mention our honeymoon,' he bit out tautly. 'I would hardly tell my mother we rarely left the bedroom!'

He made even that sound like an insult! 'Why not?' she snapped. 'It's what most people do on their honeymoon!'

He gave her a look of disgust. 'Maybe I just didn't want to boast,' he taunted.

Morgan gave a disappointed sigh. The indulgent

lover from Barbados was sadly gone. The man in his place was even harder than the Alex Hammond she had known before. 'Do you really have to go to the office today?' She looked at him anxiously, sitting forward to touch his shoulder.

'I've just spent three weeks alone with you, Morgan, wasn't that enough?' he rasped scornfully.

She moved back as if he had struck her. The honeymoon really was over!

She made no demur as, once he had settled Courtney and herself into the house, Alex left almost immediately for London. He had made it more than plain that he needed to be away from her, to be with someone other than her after their seclusion. And while she missed him unbearably she understood that there were some men who needed more of a challenge in conversation and ideas than she, as a woman, was able to give. She just hadn't thought Alex was one of those men . . .

Courtney kept the rest of her day occupied. He was taking an interest in things about him now, able to concentrate for short periods of time as she played with a toy with him, and he fell asleep as she softly sang to him.

'Mr Hammond called about ten minutes ago, madam,' the middle-aged housekeeper Alex had employed told her as she came downstairs. 'When I told him you were with the baby he said not to disturb you.'

'Did he leave a message?' she asked impatiently, wishing she could have talked to Alex herself, wanting desperately to bridge the gulf that had yawned between them.

'He said he had been delayed in London, and—and for you not to wait dinner for him,' Mrs Whitney smiled with relief as she finished reciting the message.

'Thank you,' Morgan said dully. Suddenly she had

lost her own appetite. 'Don't bother with dinner then, Mrs Whitney. I'll have something later if I get hungry.' But she knew she wouldn't, the thought of eating nauseated her.

She was totally bewildered by Alex's coldness, this not wanting to be with her. An afternoon at work she could perhaps accept, but an evening too! No, she didn't believe for a moment that Alex was staying in London this evening on business.

He hadn't returned at ten-thirty when she had given Courtney his late night feed and settled him down until morning, having got to the stage, at six weeks, where he slept through. She decided she might as well go to bed herself. Alex might not come back at all tonight!

Their bedroom had been decorated in a soft green and cream, very restful, and yet Morgan didn't feel in the least sleepy. How could Alex do this to her on their first evening in their new home! Anger took over from hurt, and by the time she heard the Mercedes coming down the driveway and pull up outside the house she was at boiling point. She would not be treated like this!

She was standing in the middle of the room when she heard Alex's ascent up the stairs, her black nightgown clinging seductively to her rose-tipped breasts, the sheerness of the material clearly showing the rest of her body. If Alex expected her to be the sort of wife who cowed in bed pretending to be asleep rather than risk confrontation then he was mistaken; she wasn't the one arriving home at eleven o'clock at night after supposedly going to the office!

Alex came to a halt in the doorway as he saw her standing proudly in front of him. 'Morgan,' he drawled, then recovered quickly, closing the door quietly and coming in to remove his tie. 'I thought you'd be asleep,' he raised dark brows questioningly.

'Did you?' she snapped. 'I wouldn't have thought you'd had the time to think of me at all—or that you would want to.'

His mouth tightened. 'Morgan——'

She glared at him with sparkling green eyes. 'If you want to discontinue the physical side of our marriage, Alex, then just say so,' she told him abruptly. 'If I failed to give you pleasure then tell me so. You don't have to stay out of your own home just to avoid me. I—Oh!' she gasped as she was pulled roughly into his arms.

'Discontinue the physical side of our marriage!' he repeated fiercely, shaking her. 'You can talk in such a businesslike way of the explosion of the senses we share?' he grated.

'You seem to want it businesslike,' she choked emotionally.

'I want *you*. *God* . . .!' he groaned as he pulled her against his chest. 'You give me pleasure unspeakable, unimaginable. And I wasn't avoiding you,' he spoke into the softness of her hair. 'At least, not voluntarily. I was giving *you* the chance to end the physical relationship, to end the honeymoon if you wanted to.' He pulled back to look at her tear-wet face. 'You don't want to, do you?' he realised huskily.

'Never!' She buried her face against his chest. 'I want you so much!'

'And I want you,' he admitted savagely, stripping off their clothes without concern for their welfare, tearing them if they wouldn't come off quickly enough, taking her fiercely, possessively, but knowing she was with him every minute, that she even revelled in his savagery.

CHAPTER EIGHT

FOR a woman who had been married a little over two months Morgan had a glow about her that made her blush whenever she happened to catch sight of her reflection in a mirror. Two months of being Alex's wife, of spending every night in his arms, bathed in his never-ending lovemaking, had given her a happiness she could hardly believe was possible.

There had been no repeats of their first evening back, no more late nights in London or anywhere else. She had never questioned Alex as to his whereabouts that night, and he had never offered the information. It was enough for her that there were no repeats of it.

And Courtney, at three months old, seemed to react to the air of happiness that surrounded the woman he considered his mother. He was the most placid of babies, starting to smile now, loving it when his daddy played gently on the bed with him.

They were so much like any normal family, with none of the tragic circumstances that had brought them all together overshadowing the relationship, that she felt no qualms about inviting Rita Hammond over to tea one afternoon. Alex had taken Courtney over to see his mother once a week for the last six weeks since their return from Barbados, but never once had he invited her here, possibly sensing Morgan's reluctance from their last meeting.

But today she was feeling very happy with the world, and144 had invited the other woman over this afternoon for tea. Rita Hammond had seemed rather stunned yesterday on the telephone by such a formal invitation to her son's house, but she had accepted

anyway. Alex had merely raised his brows when she
told him of the invitation, a habit she had learnt meant
he was puzzled. She was a little puzzled by this
herself, had felt herself well rid of Rita Hammond the
last few weeks, but she was after all Alex's mother,
and they couldn't keep up this vendetta of hatred for
ever. At least, she couldn't; she had a feeling Rita
Hammond could, though!

Her mother-in-law arrived promptly at four-thirty
that afternoon, had driven herself over in the Rolls.
Morgan felt relieved when she saw the other woman's
appearance that she had changed for the occasion,
putting on a royal blue pants suit. Rita's pure silk
dress was an attractive shade of silver-grey, very
attractive on the older woman, although Morgan eyed
the expensive dress with a sense of unease. She had
learnt that although she liked to dress attractively
herself it wasn't always wise to dress expensively, not
with a young baby about. Obviously Rita Hammond
had forgotten what it was like when her children were
babies!

The other woman looked critically about the lounge,
at the rust-coloured suite, the mottled gold carpet,
rust-coloured curtains, the beautifully ornate coffee-
table, several lamps placed about the room. Morgan
tried to see the room through the other woman's eyes;
and could find no fault with it.

'You have an attractive home, at least,' Rita said
grudgingly after several awkward minutes. 'You had
professional help with the décor, no doubt.'

'No,' Morgan smiled at the other woman's attempt
to belittle what she had done with the house. 'Before I
became an actress I studied interior decorating.'

'How useful!' Rita said disdainfully.

'Yes. Would you like me to bring Courtney down
now?'

'Well, that is why I'm here!'

She raised mocking brows. 'I thought you were here for tea,' she derided before going upstairs to get Courtney as he awakened from his nap. She was glad she could find something amusing about Rita's attitude; she had a feeling she was going to need a sense of humour during this visit from her mother-in-law.

Luckily Courtney managed to bridge some of the awkwardness, both women obviously doting on him. They watched in amusement as he lay on the floor moving his arms and legs about in an effort to crawl, becoming red-faced with anger as he didn't move a fraction of an inch.

'The exercise is good for him,' Morgan said laughingly as she gathered the baby up in her arms, soothing his indignant wails, almost as if he had been sure he had been about to crawl if she hadn't picked him up. 'It will strengthen his muscles, the health visitor told me.' She nuzzled into Courtney's neck, soon hearing his delighted gurgles.

'I have no doubt about Courtney's health,' Rita said haughtily. 'I'm just wondering when you're going to tire of this latest role.'

Morgan blinked her surprise. 'Role?'

'As doting wife and mother,' the other woman derided. 'You may be a competent actress, but how much longer do you think you'll be able to keep up the act?'

She drew in a steadying breath. 'Mrs Hammond, I invited you here today to have tea and visit Courtney, that doesn't entitle you to insult me.'

'I merely asked——'

'An impertinent and ridiculous question!' Morgan stood up in her agitation, Courtney clinging to her hair as he sensed her anger. 'I am not *acting* as Alex's wife and Courtney's mother, I *am* both those things. I would have thought that by now you would have been able to forget your prejudice and accept me as such.'

'I've suffered you only because my son has chosen

to ruin his life by marrying you,' Rita Hammond scorned haughtily, 'and because you have joint control of my only grandson. Otherwise I wouldn't give you the time of day!' Two bright spots of colour flared in her cheeks as she glared her dislike. 'I'm well aware that it's been your influence that has prevented my son inviting me to his own home, that you have also prevented my seeing Courtney as often as I would like——'

'Alex brings him over every week!' she gasped.

'For half an hour,' the other woman dismissed. 'Not nearly long enough.'

'Too long, I think,' remarked a dangerously soft voice.

Both women turned in the direction of that voice, Alex standing in the open doorway.

'Alex darling——' his mother held out pleading hands to him.

'Mother,' he bit out a cold greeting, crossing the room to Morgan's side, putting an arm possessively about her shoulders, drawing her against his side as he felt her tremble.

'Your mother was just leaving,' Morgan told him challengingly.

He nodded grimly. 'So I gathered,' he said tautly.

'Alex, you can't mean it!' his mother gasped her outrage. 'I'm your mother! I——'

'And Morgan is my wife,' he rasped harshly. 'I will not have you or anyone else insulting her—and you might as well pass that on to Janet too.'

'Janet?' his mother frowned.

'You're two of a kind, Mother,' he derided harshly. 'But this time you've gone too far—you've voiced your insults against Morgan in front of me. Morgan has done her best to protect both you and Janet from my knowing the exact nature of your vindictiveness—Oh yes, she's done that,' he nodded grimly at his mother's snort of disbelief. 'But after listening to you just now, to the lies you actually believe, I think she was wrong to do that. I made no mistake when I married Morgan, Mother,' he told her coldly. 'And it had nothing to do with Morgan that you haven't been invited here before, I didn't want it. "

'You?' his mother gasped again. 'I can't believe that, Alex——'

'Believe it,' he bit out ruthlessly. 'And believe this too, Mother. My marriage to Morgan is completely successful. Completely,' he repeated harshly. 'The last thing I wanted was your coming here and disrupting that. But you have,' his fingers bit painfully into Morgan's shoulder in his anger. 'Now I second Morgan's request that you leave.' He seemed not to notice Morgan's gasp of surprise. 'And I don't want to see you here again until you feel you can apologise to my wife for the insults you've given her both today and in the past.'

'Never!' came his mother's instant—and expected— reply.

He turned away from her, to ring for Mrs Whitney. 'Then we have nothing more to say to each other. Ah, Mrs Whitney,' his voice softened to politeness as the housekeeper came in answer to his call. 'My mother is just leaving.'

'Alex——'

'Goodbye, Mother.' His voice was uncompromising.

She shot an impatient glance at the waiting housekeeper. 'You'll regret this,' was all she could bring herself to say in front of a servant.

'I don't think so,' he replied confidently as his mother marched out of the room and out of the house.

'God . . .!' Morgan shuddered as reaction began to set in, the scene the ugliest yet.

'Give Courtney to me,' Alex prompted gently.

She gave him the baby, then buried her face in her

shaking hands. 'Why does she hate me so much?' she choked.

He shrugged. 'She just can't bear to see anyone else happy.'

'You mean no woman is good enough for her sons!' Morgan snapped.

Alex grinned. 'There's that too . . .' He sobered. 'Look, I can't ever guess the reason she dislikes you. But she will apologise to you.'

'You heard her! Never, she said.'

'She will,' he repeated grimly. 'And if she doesn't then it's her loss.' His eyes darkened. 'Can you leave Courtney with Mrs Whitney for an hour—or two?' he asked throatily.

She looked at him with a frown, wondering why on earth she should want to leave Courtney with the housekeepr. At the warmth in his gaze she knew. 'Alex!' she exclaimed in a shocked voice.

He laughed huskily. 'You were magnificent, darling. And I want to feel the fire that's built up in you. Do you mind?'

She took Courtney from him. 'I'll just go and ask Mrs Whitney to take care of him for a while.'

'Don't be long,' Alex requested throatily as she reached the door.

'Two minutes,' she promised eagerly.

She was less than that, and hurried upstairs to their bedroom to find Alex waiting for her in his bathrobe.

'I thought we could shower together,' he explained softly.

'Oh yes!' She eagerly took off her own clothes.

Alex watched her with appreciative eyes. 'What did you tell Mrs Whitney?'

Morgan moved about the bedroom with unconscious grace, knowing that Alex loved to see her nakedness. 'I told her we have a few things to discuss and that the baby might be a distraction,' she laughed softly.

Alex returned that smile, curving her nakedness against him, murmuring his agreement as she untied the belt to his robe, then stepping inside the garment to press herself against him. 'I have quite a lot of things I would like to—discuss with you,' he said softly. 'And I'm not sure I can wait for the shower,' he groaned urgently, his body already hardened to passion.

'Then we won't.' She drew his head down to hers, revelling in his mastery of her, giving herself to him completely each time they made love, and knowing that little by little, Alex was slowly coming to give himself to her in return without even realising it. He always gave her pleasure, always accepted the pleasure she gave him in return, but now it was more than that, now he was starting to give some of his inner self, to reveal more and more of himself to her as they grew closer day by day.

'I wasn't expecting you home so early.' She lay on his sweat-dampened chest some time later, unwilling to break the oneness with him as she looked down at him.

'Are you complaining?' he taunted with lazy satisfaction, pushing back a damp tendril from her forehead.

'Are you?' she mocked from her dominant position above him.

Alex laughed throatily. 'I never complain when you become aggressive. I love it!'

She wished he could have been saying that he loved her, but maybe in time that would come too. 'Why did you come home so early?' she persisted. 'It was only five o'clock, and you don't usually get home until at least six o'clock.'

'I was thinking of you, and had to get home before I raped my secretary in my frustration!'

'Alex, Miss Kingsley is fifty years old!'

He grinned. 'I know. Think how shocked she would have been!'

'Alex . . .!' She gave him a stern look as he once again evaded her question.

'Okay,' he sighed. 'I had a feeling my mother might try her Lady of the Manor act.' He shrugged. 'I had no intention of letting her get away with it again.'

The light died out of Morgan's face as she thought of the ugly scene that had taken place just over an hour ago. 'I really thought she would be all right this time,' she sighed.

'I knew she wouldn't,' Alex drawled. 'She probably never will be.'

She remembered the determination on the other woman's face. 'She'll never apologise to me, Alex. She dislikes me too much.'

'Then as I said, she isn't welcome here again.' His tone was implacable. 'And I have no intention of going there either.'

Alex kept to his word, and during the two weeks that followed they didn't see or hear from his mother, something that didn't seem to bother him in the least, but which worried her. There was already enough friction in this family, and she didn't like being the reason for causing more. Finally it was Janet Fairchild who came to see them. Morgan hadn't forgotten that the last time the two of them had met she had struck the other woman. Janet gave no indication of remembering the incident, but Morgan had come to know the other woman well enough to know she hadn't forgotten a thing.

The three of them sat in the lounge, with the fire lit on this Saturday afternoon in early December. 'Don't you think you've punished Mother enough?' Janet drawled bluntly.

Alex raised dark brows at the description. 'Punished?' he repeated softly. 'There's no punishment intended.'

His sister gave an impatient sigh. 'Then why do you persist in staying away, in keeping Courtney from her?'

'I don't "persist" in anything,' he replied confidently. 'If Mother wants to see him all she has to do is apologise to his mother.'

Janet's eyes flashed angrily. 'Morgan is not Courtney's mother!' she snapped.

'Janet,' he drawled in a softly warning voice, 'I would hate to have to ask you to leave too.' He raised dark brows questioningly.

'Alex, please!' Morgan touched his chest pleadingly as they sat side by side on the sofa, Courtney having fallen asleep on a cushion at her other side.

Janet's mouth tightened even more. 'I don't need you to defend me!' she rasped insultingly.

Morgan knew that Alex's eyes darkened dangerously, and she turned to give the other woman a smile. 'I'm sure you don't,' she said smoothly. 'And your mother is welcome here at any time.' She felt the feud had gone on long enough.

'Not until she apologises,' Alex said harshly.

'Alex——'

'I mean it, Morgan,' he told her softly. 'Mark may have been too weak to defend his wife against his family, but I am not.'

'Mark was too weak to stop a lot of things,' Janet taunted.

Morgan stiffened, glancing anxiously at Alex. Surely the other woman wasn't going to bring up the question of Courtney's paternity in front of Alex? She would swear Alex didn't even suspect such a thing about Glenna; he always spoke of her so warmly, so without the prejudice of his mother and sister.

'Well, I'm not.' He stood up forcefully. 'So you can go home and tell Mother that this touching little plea didn't work. An apology for Morgan is what I want, and an apology is what I shall have. It's what I demand, damn it!'

His anger stayed with him for the rest of the day, but as soon as they were in bed together it gentled to exquisite adoration, and he made love to her with his usual consideration and passion.

Alex showed no surprise when his mother arrived the next day, although Morgan's heart somersaulted wildly as Mrs Whitney came into the lounge to announce her.

'Show her in,' Alex nodded, moving to stand with his foot on the hearth, an indulgent smile curving his lips as he saw Morgan's nervousness. 'Relax,' he soothed. 'She can't hurt you.'

'She can try!' she grimaced

Rita Hammond certainly didn't have the look of a woman about to apologise for anything as she swept regally into the room seconds later, her eyes flashing angrily as she looked ready to do battle.

'Good afternoon, Mother,' Alex drawled.

'Alex,' she nodded coolly. 'Morgan.' Her voice hardened even more.

The silence seemed to stretch out after these curt greetings. Alex was unwilling to bridge the awkwardness, Rita Hammond was unlikely to, and Morgan was unable to. She knew Alex was determined his mother should apologise or leave.

Hard blue eyes were finally turned on Morgan, the words seeming forced out of Rita Hammond's red-painted lips. 'I believe I owe you an apology, that you took exception to something I said——'

'*I* took exception to it,' Alex corrected hardly.

His mother flushed her displeasure. 'Very well. I'm sorry, Morgan,' she ground out, 'if anything I said to you seemed rude.'

'It didn't "seem" it, Mother,' Alex bit out. 'It was. I heard it all, remember?'

For a brief moment Morgan saw the older woman's bottom lip tremble precariously, and she realised that Rita Hammond wasn't as in control of herself as she wanted to appear. 'That's perfectly all right,' she rushed into speech, unable to bear the other woman's humiliation any longer. Alex could still be a very hard man, despite his apparent satisfaction with their marriage. 'Would you like to come up to the nursery and see how well Courtney is doing? He should be awake now.'

'Thank you,' her mother-in-law accepted huskily.

If she expected the other woman to take back her apology as soon as they were out of the room then she was disappointed, pleasantly so. They discussed only Courtney, and that in a friendly way too.

'He's grown so much in just two weeks.' Rita lifted the baby up into her arms as he lay gurgling up at them from his cot.

'Yes.' Morgan at once felt guilty, knowing it was her fault the other woman had been denied access to her grandson. 'Mrs Hammond——'

'Rita,' the other woman invited, laughing softly at Morgan's shocked expression. 'Oh, don't worry, I'm not suddenly going to turn from the Wicked Witch into the Good Fairy,' she drawled. 'I'm just wise enough to know that Alex has made the choice everyone has to make one day, that between family and a new spouse. Mark never did seem to make the transition, and that was probably my fault, but Alex is more like me than any of my children. He has made a decision, that you and Courtney come first in his life now, and I either accept that or lose you all. I'll accept it,' she added dryly.

It was the nearest to an acceptance into the Hammond family *she* was ever likely to get, and she knew that. As for coming first in Alex's life, she knew the baby did that, that despite the physical attraction between Alex and herself that he still didn't love her, that he probably never would.

Her parents flew over for Christmas, and stayed on for Courtney's christening in January. Her father was much stronger now, Courtney was all he needed to make the recovery a hundred per cent.

The christening was the first real formal occasion Morgan had hosted for Alex, and she wanted everything to be perfect for him, wanted him to be proud she was his wife. Rita had been a lot of help in the organisation of the party. The older woman had been right—they hadn't suddenly become friends, but they did tolerate each other, and Rita Hammond was much more helpful as a mother-in-law than an enemy.

The church service was short and beautiful, and even when the water was dribbled over his head Courtney didn't cry.

'He reminded me so much of you at that moment, Alex,' Morgan's mother laughed softly later at the house, her parents and Alex having become good friends the last three weeks during their visit. 'He looked positively indignant!' she chuckled.

Morgan held back her own smile as Alex's brows rose, knowing that her husband had been the recipient of a lot of teasing while her parents had been here, his English reserve amusing them. It amused her too, and yet she knew that when it came to making love Alex wasn't reserved at all.

'He probably wondered what on earth was going on,' he drawled, glancing at the sleeping baby in his carrycot. 'He isn't even going to know that we're about to toast him in champagne.'

'We are?' Morgan's eyes widened.

'A gift from your father,' he nodded. 'I'll go and organise it.'

He strode off towards the kitchen, tall and attractive in a navy blue suit and constrasting lighter blue shirt.

Morgan watched him with pride—she would give up a hundred parts like Mary-Beth to be his wife. The series had been shown over here the last few months, and her death as Mary-Beth had shocked a lot of the public. What they couldn't realise was the happiness she had found as Morgan Hammond. She shivered with the anticipation of sharing a bed with Alex that night, knowing that tonight, as every other night since they were married, Alex would make love to her until she was mindless.

She looked around the room with the critical eye of the hostess, checking that everyone had food and drink, that no one was sitting in a corner being bored. Everyone looked happy enough—

Her gaze was caught and held by belligerent blue eyes—Janet Fairchild's eyes! The other woman stood slightly across the room from her, her mouth twisted sardonically.

Morgan never felt comfortable about Alex's sister; she always sensed that the other woman was just waiting for something, the right time, and she was going to strike, and strike hard. It was a ridiculous feeling, the other woman's manner was always pleasant, and the day they had spent with them over Christmas had been enjoyable. And yet that unease persisted . . .

Janet was smiling at her now, the dislike gone from her face, making Morgan wonder if she had just imagined the venom there to start with.

'Champagne, darling?'

She turned to look at her husband, accepting the champagne he held out to her, used to the casual words of endearment he gave her now. She smiled at him warmly, Janet forgotten as the toast was given to Courtney.

When Courtney woke up he was passed from guest to guest to be duly admired, looking quite affronted by all these different people admiring him; as if he needed anyone else's opinion on how wonderful he was!

'Your mother was right.' Janet suddenly stood at Morgan's side, still sipping at her glass of champagne. 'Courtney does have Alex's air of breeding. And that wasn't meant to be insulting,' she drawled with amusement. 'Heaven forbid that Alex should order me from the house!'

Morgan felt that feeling of unease return. 'I'm sure it wasn't,' she returned smoothly.

Janet strolled over to the window, looking up at the grey sky. 'They forecast snow for today,' she murmured thoughtfully. 'It looks as if they might actually be right for once!'

Morgan moved to stand next to the other woman. 'Yes,' she agreed softly, still wary.

Hard blue eyes were turned on her. 'Your parents return home soon, don't they?'

She felt a sense of sadness, and nodded slowly. 'In two days' time.'

'Obviously you'll miss them.'

'Obviously,' she agreed, more than ever wary of this seemingly pleasant conversation with a woman who seemed to dislike her intensely.

'Still, you have Alex—and my mother.'

'Yes,' Morgan was frowning now. Janet hadn't spoke to her this much since her wedding day, and they both knew how that conversation had ended!

'My mother came round beautifully, didn't she?' said Janet with humour—only Morgan doubted the other woman was genuinely amused. The humour was hard, mocking, not friendly at all. 'But then you have her grandson,' she added softly.

'Janet, I don't think——'

'This is the place to discuss this,' Janet finished dryly. 'Are you happy with my brother, Morgan?'

Her gaze went instinctively to her husband, love lighting her eyes as she watched him charming her parents, looking up as if he sensed her gaze on him, giving her a warm smile before Courtney attracted his attention from his position of pride in his grand-mother's arms.

'Of course you are,' Janet answered her own question. 'And he and Courtney look so right together, don't they, almost like father and son.'

'Janet——'

'But then maybe that's because they probably are,' Janet continued softly.

Morgan's face was suddenly pale as the words sank in, her eyes huge with disbelief. 'Wh-what did you say?' Her mouth felt dry, her tongue cleaved to the roof of her mouth, she was sure that she couldn't have heard the other woman properly. What she was saying was insane!

'You want me to say the words again?' the other woman scorned. 'I won't bother to say it, Morgan, I don't need to—just look at the two of them together. Look!' she ordered sharply as Morgan averted her face. 'The same wavy hair, the same grey eyes, the same high cheekbones, even the same determined chin,' she listed the similarity in features that was all too obvious now to even the most casual observer.

And Morgan was far from being that! The similarities were all too obvious to her too—now that this vindictive woman had pointed them out! Except for the colour of his hair, that soft red down, at four months Courtney was almost a mirror image of Alex. But his *son*? No, she couldn't believe that, *wouldn't* believe it.

CHAPTER NINE

'I SHOULD, Morgan,' Janet drawled, guessing her thoughts. 'Because it's the truth.'

'No . . .!' Morgan choked, so white now she was almost grey, her eyes like huge emeralds in her face, the black of her dress making her skin appear translucent.

'Morgan?' Alex suddenly appeared at her side, looking down at her anxiously. 'Darling, what is it?' he frowned, clasping her hands in his.

'She isn't feeling too well.' Janet was the one to answer him. 'It's very warm in here, with the fire going and all these people. I'll take her upstairs and she can lie down for a while.'

His arm went about Morgan's shoulders. 'I'll take her.'

'No!' she wrenched away from him. 'I—No,' she moved away from him, looking at him as if she had never seen him before.

'I'll take her,' Janet offered smoothly. 'You have your guests to take care of, Alex, you can't both desert them.'

Alex seemed undecided, looking from his sister to Morgan with a puzzled frown.

'Graham and Sheila are just leaving,' Janet urged him to stay.

He glanced round. 'I'll have to go to them.' He looked down at Morgan. 'Will you be all right for a while? I'll come up to you as soon as everyone has gone.'

'I—I'll be fine.' She just had to get out of here

before she made a fool of herself and asked him straight out if what Janet had told her was the truth. 'I'll just go and lie down.' She turned and almost ran out of the room, not giving Alex a second look in her need to escape.

It wasn't until she reached the bedroom she shared with Alex that she realised Janet had followed her. 'I'd rather be alone,' she halted the other woman at the door, her expression determined.

Janet raised dark brows. 'Don't you want to know the rest of it, of Alex's affair with Glenna?'

'I don't believe you——'

'Then why did you flinch away from Alex a few seconds ago?' the other woman taunted, and pushed the door open with ease, following Morgan into the room as she backed dazedly to the bed, sitting down abruptly. 'I told you there'd been another man, Morgan,' she continued in that mocking voice. 'Didn't you ever think of Alex? He was so convenient, and Glenna was so beautiful.'

'No . . .!' Morgan groaned, closing her eyes as if to block out this nightmare.

'Yes!' Janet hissed. 'Why do you think Alex was so determined to keep Courtney in England? Why do you think he married *you*?' she added scornfully. 'You're beautiful enough, I grant you that. You even have a surface resemblance to Glenna. Why, in the dark I don't suppose——'

'Stop it! *Stop it!*' Morgan stood up fiercely, her hands clenched at her sides. 'I don't want to hear any more.'

'Well, that's too bad, because I intend telling you all of it. You see, Glenna was very unhappy here, and Alex was always kind to her. It was inevitable that Glenna would turn to him when Mark looked like becoming bored with her.'

'It's a lie!' Her eyes sparkled like emeralds. 'Alex

would never do such a thing where his own brother was involved!'

Janet's mouth twisted contemptuously. 'Where sex is involved a man has no scruples, not even Alex.'

Morgan turned away. She would not believe this! Janet hated her for some reason, wanted to hurt her. And yet Alex *was* the only one who had spoken kindly about Glenna, the only one who had really seemed to like her.

'Think about it, Morgan,' the other woman encouraged softly. 'Just think about it.'

She didn't want to think at all, but she could do nothing else after Janet had left. She knew it must be a lie, and yet the nagging doubt persisted. Alex *had* refused to let Courtney leave England, and while his reason that Courtney shouldn't become a tug-of-love child still seemed a valid enough one for them to marry, the fact that Courtney was his son was an even stronger one.

And the thought of him imagining she was Glenna when they made love made her feel sick! They rarely talked when they made love, just enjoyed each other's bodies, and she suspected even that now. Maybe if they spoke he would realise she wasn't Glenna and not want her any more. Oh, it was all so insane, and yet *it could be the truth*!

They had agreed on total honesty in their marriage, and so far Morgan had given Alex that, but *this*—this she couldn't talk to him about. Because she feared the answer! It would destroy her and the marriage to know she was merely a substitute for her sister.

She was lying on the bed white-faced and dry-eyed when Alex came into the bedroom an hour later, and she looked up at him with searching eyes as he sat down beside her on the bed. She had come to love this man so much during the three months of their marriage, couldn't imagine a life without him, he had become so much a part of her in that short time. And yet he still gave away none of his own feelings, not even at their most intimate moments, and those inner feelings were what she needed at this moment to tell her that she was Morgan, his wife, and not a substitute for Glenna, his lover.

'They've all gone,' he told her softly, smoothing back her hair. 'Does your head hurt?' he frowned.

'Head hurt?' Amazingly she could still talk, and quite normally too! She had felt sure she would never be able to talk to him normally again.

His mouth quirked. 'You're lying here in the dark.'

'Oh.' She hadn't even realised it was dark!

'Everyone left early because of the snow.' He leant over and switched on the dimmed bedside lamp. 'It's coming down quite heavily now. And, of course, the party fell quite flat without its beautiful hostess.'

She turned her head away. 'I'm sorry.'

'Hey, I'm only teasing,' he said, gently turning her face towards him. 'Although everyone was concerned,' he frowned once again. 'Including me.'

'I—It's just a sick headache. The excitement of Christmas and now the christening, I expect.'

His brows drew together. 'Is that all it is? Janet hasn't been putting her little daggers in again, has she?'

'Janet?' Her voice was lightly brittle.

'You suddenly stopped feeling well when she was talking to you,' Alex drawled.

'Sick headaches are like that,' she told him. 'They come on suddenly.'

'Hm,' he didn't sound convinced. 'Do you feel well enough to see your parents? They're worried about you.'

'Er—I'd rather not. I'd like to take a nap. Could you explain to them?' She looked at him appealingly, knowing she couldn't face anyone right now.

'Of course,' he comforted. 'Shall I bring Courtney in to say goodnight to you?'

'I have to put him to bed——'

'I'm sure your mother and I can manage for one night,' he said dryly. 'I realise it's over the month's trial, and that you've been doing very well with him, but are you sure it isn't caring for Courtney that's caused this headache? You've been up in the night to him several times lately.'

Before this talk with Janet Morgan would have been warmed by his concern for her, now she wasn't so sure it wasn't just for his son's welfare, that he wanted the very best for him. She was allowing Janet's unbelievable statement to cloud her behaviour in spite of herself, and she was unable to stop her next snapped comment. 'Other mothers do it. I'm not made of porcelain, Alex!' Her mouth was tight.

He looked surprised by her outburst; her temperament had been far from argumentative since they had been married. 'I know that, darling,' he said slowly. 'I just didn't want you to wear yourself out with him, make yourself ill.'

'I have a headache, Alex,' she told him impatiently. 'I'm not exactly ill!'

'All right, Morgan.' His tone was gentle, his hand even more so as he touched her cheek. 'I'll bring Courtney in to see you and then you can get some sleep.'

But she couldn't sleep at all. Thoughts kept crowding her mind, images of herself and Alex as they made love, the terrible agony of wondering if it wasn't her he saw at all but Glenna.

Somehow the idea that Alex was the man involved made her doubt her sister's ability to have an affair less. Alex was so attractive, devastatingly so, and when he made love he cared nothing for his own pleasure until he was sure she had reached the peak of her own fulfilment. He was a completely unselfish lover, and to a woman in an unhappy marriage that could be a strong temptation.

She refused any dinner, taking a shower and getting into bed, desperately trying to get to sleep before Alex came to bed too. She wasn't sure she could bear his hands on her tonight, the joy she had felt this afternoon at the thought of making love with him had completely gone now.

She was still awake as he came quietly into their bedroom after taking his shower, and she heard him moving softly about the room preparing for bed. She was dreading the moment he got into bed beside her, and felt herself stiffen as his thigh brushed against the back of hers as he slid in next to her.

'Morgan?' He touched her shoulder lightly.

She closed her eyes at the sensation of longing that washed over her at the feel of his hand on her flesh, sensing his puzzlement as he realised a silky nightgown covered her body; she hadn't hidden her nakedness from him since their wedding night.

'Morgan?' His voice sharpened as he rolled her over to face him. 'Are you cold, darling?' he asked softly as he looked into her opened eyes.

Cold? She was *frozen*, her emotions numb! 'A little,' she said huskily.

He pulled her into his arms, her face against his chest as his lips moved across her shoulder. 'Let me warm you,' he murmured throatily.

'Not tonight, Alex,' she pushed against him, her eyes dark with pain as he looked down at her. 'I still have a headache, and I—I——'

'It's all right, Morgan,' he soothed teasingly. 'I'm not going to hold one headache against you, not after three months. I'll just hold you tonight, hmm?'

She couldn't even bear that! 'I'm feeling hot now, Alex,' she said evasively. 'I think I'll just lie over my side of the bed. Maybe I'm coming down with another cold.'

'Maybe.' He released her slowly, reluctantly. 'Are you sure you aren't upset about something?'

'Of course not,' she answered sharply. 'I can't be in the mood for sex every night, Alex!'

'No,' he bit out, lying on his back, his head turned towards her. 'I think we're getting to the truth of it now, aren't we, Morgan? I accept that perhaps you aren't feeling well, but that's never stopped us in the past. Tonight you won't even let me hold you, and now you say it's because you aren't in the mood. Which is it, Morgan, feeling ill, or not in the mood?' he derided harshly.

Her mouth set angrily. 'Not in the mood!'

'That's what I thought,' he snapped, turning his back on her. 'Goodnight!'

She hadn't wanted to argue with him, and she lay miserably on her side of the bed, knowing by the even tenor of his breathing that Alex had soon fallen asleep. She couldn't stand to be apart from him any more, she needed his warmth, and she edged over the bed until she was curved into the back of him, her arm about his waist as her head rested on his back. She gave a deep sigh of pleasure and curled more comfortably against him, asleep within seconds.

She was alone when she woke up, despite the earliness of the hour, dressing quickly before going into Courtney's room next door to take him down for his morning feed. The nursery was empty.

Courtney was in the breakfast-room with Alex, neither of her parents being awake yet. A blush stole into her cheeks as she looked at her husband; she was wary of his mood this morning.

He looked back at her with cool grey eyes, finishing his coffee before standing up. 'How are you feeling this morning?' he asked distantly.

'Better, thank you.' Her own manner was as cool.

He nodded. 'Courtney has been fed. You were sleeping so deeply when he woke I didn't like to disturb you.'

'Thank you,' she said once again, picking up the baby. 'I'll give him his bath now.'

'Have some breakfast first,' he instructed.

Her mouth tightened at his autocratic attitude. 'I don't want any,' she told him curtly.

'You had no dinner last night either.' He looked at her sternly. 'We wouldn't want you to be really ill, now would we?' he added tauntingly.

Her flush was one of anger this time. She couldn't believe that the closeness she and Alex had built up over three months of marriage could be destroyed by just one small argument because she didn't want to make love. Was that all their marriage consisted of, physical gratification?

'I said I'm not hungry,' she bit out tautly. 'Excuse me,' and she swept out of the room.

'Morgan!' Alex's voice stopped her part way up the stairs.

She turned slowly. 'Yes?'

'Take it easy today, hmm?' His tone was gentle, a question in his puzzled eyes.

Her anger faded as quickly as it had risen; she was filled with confusion now, loving this man in spite of what Janet had told her. 'I—Yes.' She made her way quickly to the nursery, refusing to think, intending to keep herself occupied so that she didn't have the time to brood.

If her parents wondered at her burst of energy they didn't say anything. The three of them were enjoying this last day of their vacation. Her parents were taking the midday flight back to California the next day. It was going to be difficult to part from her parents after their three-week stay, and she knew they weren't looking forward to parting from their new grandson; both of them were falling under Courtney's undoubted charm.

'Morgan and I will probably bring him over during the summer,' Alex told them that evening once Courtney had been put to bed, and the love and heartache in their faces at parting from him was enough to move even the hardest heart.

Nevertheless, Morgan was surprised by this information; Alex hadn't mentioned it to her before.

'A surprise for you,' he told her indulgently at her raised eyebrows. 'I thought we could get away for a month in July.'

His mood had been pleasant since his arrival home from the office just after six. He had come into their bedroom where she was changing for dinner, kissing her warmly on the mouth, the argument last night and the coldness of this morning forgotten as he kissed her with complete thoroughness.

'Do we have time——' he broke off as Courtney let out a loud wail from next door. 'We don't have time,' he grimaced. 'I think our son wants you.'

She had left him then to go to Courtney, glad that she didn't have to pointedly evade going to bed with him; she knew she couldn't have let him make love to her. Not thinking today might have put off the pain, but it hadn't changed the fact that having Alex make love to her and imagine she was Glenna made her want to run away and hide. In a way she had done exactly that, spending the time until dinner in the nursery, only coming down when the others had come in to say goodnight to the baby, her parents' presence meaning she didn't have to be alone with Alex. Now he had dropped this bombshell.

'That would be lovely.' She gave him a strained smile.

'I thought so,' he nodded, watching her closely. 'As

long as Sharon and Court think they can stand to have the three of us around for all that time!' he teased her parents.

He and her parents, much to her surprise, had become firm friends during this visit, and her father's reply was predictable.

'Stay two months if you want, son,' he said warmly. 'Sharon and I would be glad to have you.'

'A month is all I can spare this time,' Alex said regretfully. 'But maybe next time we can stay longer.'

Next time. It reminded Morgan only too forcibly that her marriage to Alex was a permanent thing, and that it was a normal marriage through her own choosing, her own *demand*. Alex had told her she could opt out of that any time she wanted to, and yet to do that would end what marriage they had, end the only closeness they had.

'Any time you can get away,' her mother invited enthusiastically. 'We can't tell you what a wonderful time we've had here with you, how lovely it's been to see you all. When Morgan told us she was getting married, and to Mark's brother—well, we——'

'Were naturally concerned,' Alex finished softly. 'I can understand that. I hope that seeing us together you're convinced that we're married because we want to be, that I'm not a wife-beater,' he smiled.

'When Morgan was younger—not much younger, I might add,' her father's eyes glowed with merriment as he teased her, 'she deserved more than a few beatings. She had the temper of a shrew!'

Alex looked at her with amused eyes. 'Really?' he encouraged.

Her father settled comfortably into the role of revealing her childhood antics. 'She was such a tomboy, always climbing trees, scuffing her knees. The complaints we had from the neighbours!' he chuckled. 'Morgan was always bringing home stray animals that would go and dig up their gardens.'

'Dad!' she warned.

'Tell me more,' Alex grinned. 'It doesn't sound at all like my elegant wife.'

Morgan had to suffer the indignity of all her childhood exploits being told to Alex as they ate dinner, his throaty laugh often bubbling to the surface. To all intents and purposes they were a happy family circle, and no one seemed aware of Morgan's shattered emotions. She could put on an act for one day, maybe even a week, but how was she going to get through the rest of her life like this!

'I'm going to miss your parents,' Alex murmured as he undressed later that night, pulling off his tie and unbuttoning his shirt. 'I've enjoyed having them here.'

Morgan kept her face averted, continuing to brush her hair in front of the mirror, the lime green nightgown fitting smoothly over her breasts and thighs. 'I'm sure they've enjoyed being here,' she nodded.

Alex came to stand behind her in the mirror, his chest bare now, his black trousers low down on his hips. It was impossible to do anything else but look at his reflection, her gaze held mesmerised by his physical perfection. His hands came down on her shoulders as he knelt slightly on the back of her stool, his head bent as his mouth nuzzled her nape.

'How do you feel today?' he asked softly.

'I——' she was stopped from answering by a whimper of pain from the nursery. 'Courtney!' She evaded Alex's touch and stood up. 'He's been upset all day,' she frowned. 'I'll go to him.'

Alex followed her through to the adjoining nursery, leaning against the doorframe as Morgan picked up the baby and began to soothe him. 'What do you think it is?' he asked worriedly.

'He had his routine injection on Friday,' she shrugged, the baby's cry quietening to a choked sob. 'I think he just has a slight fever from it.'

'Should he have that?'

'Of course he should!' she snapped angrily. 'There's nothing wrong with him. Why don't you just go away?' All the tension of the day built up within her and exploded in one angry outburst. 'He'll be perfectly all right with me. Go back to bed!'

'But if he's ill——'

'He's just fretful, the nurse said he could be.'

'All right, then,' he answered angrily. 'I think I will go back to bed, as you're so confident you know what to do!' He closed the communicating door with suppressed violence.

Morgan sat down in the rocking chair with Courtney, softly thanking him for saving her from another open confrontation with Alex as to why she wouldn't let him make love to her. Because she wouldn't have been able to, she knew that as soon as he touched her.

She stayed with Courtney a lot longer than necessary, wanting to give Alex time to fall asleep. Courtney had settled down again in only minutes after she had soothed him, so she sat beside his crib for over an hour just watching him sleep. He no longer seemed hot as he had earlier in the day, so she thought the slight reaction to the injection had probably passed.

She couldn't hear any movement from the adjoining bedroom to tell her if Alex was awake or not, so she left it a little while longer, giving him time to fall into a deep sleep.

Suddenly the door between the two rooms opened and a harsh-faced Alex stood there. 'Come to bed, Morgan,' he rasped harshly. 'I won't touch you!'

'Alex——'

'Just come to bed,' he ordered bitterly, turning on his heel and walking back into the darkness, leaving the door open. 'Morgan!' he ground out.

She stood up, tucking the blanket more firmly around the sleeping baby before going slowly into the bedroom she shared with Alex. He lay far over his side of the bed, his back turned towards her in silent reproach.

She slept restlessly, somehow managing to keep away from Alex even when she did doze, waking up with a start the one time she sensed herself moving across the bed towards him. Daylight was breaking as she opened her eyes, and after the lapse she had just had she daren't fall asleep again, but lay awake until she heard Courtney's early morning cry, and hurried to his room before he woke Alex, wanting no recriminating conversations this morning.

She didn't see her husband until breakfast time. The four of them breakfasted together, Alex having taken a day off work so that he could drive her parents to the airport. It was a thoughtful gesture, and one Morgan knew her parents appreciated. Unfortunately it also meant she had his company for the entire day, and by his frosty manner towards her she knew she was far from forgiven for the last two nights of avoiding his touch.

Her mother came into the nursery to help her dress Courtney for the drive. 'He's so much like Glenna,' she said tearfully.

All Morgan could see in the baby was Alex, but she nodded anyway, concentrating on the tiny button at the neck of the sweater Courtney wore.

'We really have enjoyed being here, Morgan.' Her mother took the baby as Morgan cleared away the baby's toiletries. 'Alex has made us so welcome. And it's so nice to see how happy you are together.' She played with Courtney as she talked, so she didn't notice how pale Morgan was. 'I must say your father and I felt some serious misgivings when you and Alex decided to get married—we wondered if it wasn't just for Courtney's sake even though you told us you loved Alex. And that would have been disastrous.'

'Yes,' she agreed dully.

'But anyone can see how happy the two of you are together,' her mother smiled. 'We're so pleased for you, Morgan.'

'Yes,' she smiled again.

'I still can't say I like the rest of the family,' her mother grimaced. 'But at least Alex had the sense not to stay in the same house as his mother.'

'Yes. We'd better be going down, Mom,' Morgan suggested lightly. 'We don't have too long to get to the airport.' She hated deceiving her mother like this, but the pain of her discovery was so new she couldn't talk to anyone about it.

She sat in the back of the Mercedes with her mother and Courtney, her father seated beside Alex, although she was aware of his gaze on her often in the driving mirror, as if her behaviour the last two days was bothering him.

And no wonder—her coldness now was the complete antithesis of her manner with him the last three months. She had always been pleased to see him, to be with him, to make love with him, and now she couldn't even bare his touch, evading his hands as he would have helped her out of the car with Courtney when they reached the airport.

His eyes flashed with anger before he turned to help her father with the luggage.

Heathrow Airport was hardly the place for a tearful farewell, but as her parents went through Customs Morgan couldn't stop herself from bursting into tears, accepting the comfort of Alex's arm about her shoulders, unable to reject him in her desolation. She suddenly felt very much alone, alien, as if her parents departure had left her in a vacuum.

'Would you like Mrs Whitney to take care of

Courtney this evening?' Alex offered on the drive home. 'We could go out to dinner.'

'No!' She swallowed hard, biting back her vehemence. 'I don't want to leave Courtney just yet, not when he hasn't been well the last two days,' she said more calmly.

'I just thought you might be feeling a bit of anti-climax now that your parents have gone.' He shrugged. 'Courtney is well enough today, isn't he?' he frowned.

'Well . . . yes. But I just want to give it one more day to make sure.'

'I was only thinking of you.'

'I know—and I'm grateful. I just——'

'Don't want to be alone with me,' he finished grimly. 'What have I done, Morgan?' He turned to look at her, an expression of bewilderment in his eyes. 'I thought you were happy with me, that we were happy *together*.'

'We are,' she nodded, avoiding his gaze.

'Then why—Never mind,' he bit out impatiently. 'I can guess!'

'Guess what?' She blinked at him.

'It isn't important,' he dismissed harshly.

But it was, very important—she knew that. She was destroying what closeness they had by her silence, and yet to question Alex, to be told the truth, could destroy *her*.

For the first time since they had been married Alex spent the evening in his study working. At least, that was what he said he was doing, and Morgan didn't doubt that he could find work to do, but she knew it wasn't the necessity to work that had influenced his decision. He was avoiding her too now.

They were still avoiding each other when they went to bed early that night, each using the bathroom in silence. Alex was wearing the black silk pyjama trousers now, and Morgan's own nightgown was more than adequate covering.

He didn't even attempt to touch her as they lay side by side in the bed, neither of them talking but neither of them asleep either. Alex punched his pillow into a more comfortable position from time to time, but other than that his broad back was presented to her in cold silence.

Morgan tried to hold back her tears, knowing that if he heard her sobs he would demand an explanation right now. But the tears refused to remain checked, falling silently down her cheeks and wetting her pillow.

'This is damned ridiculous!' Alex suddenly exploded, making Morgan jump with the fierceness of his mood, then he pulled her over on to her back, looming over her in the darkness. 'I can't—Morgan, you're crying!' he groaned as he felt her tears with his thumb tips. 'Darling, what is it?' he demanded gently. 'What's wrong with you? Tell me and we can work it out.'

She shook her head, sobbing in earnest now, putting up no resistance as he pulled her close against his chest, clinging to him unashamedly.

'Morgan, speak to me!' he groaned into her hair. 'Tell me what I've done.'

'Nothing. You've done nothing,' she choked.

'Then why are you crying?' He smoothed her hair back from her face, drying her cheeks with his fingers. 'I've behaved badly the last two days,' he sighed. 'You're entitled to say no if you want to.' His eyes darkened. 'But I just can't do without you, I need you all the time. Darling . . .!' he lowered his head with a groan.

For several seconds she let him kiss her, and then she couldn't stand it any more, wondering if he were imagining she were Glenna. She pushed against his chest, twisting her face aside to wrench her mouth from his. 'No!' It was like the cry of a wounded animal.

Alex was breathing hard as he looked down at her. 'No?'

She shook her head silently, the tears flowing anew as she looked up at him.

He closed his eyes for several long painful seconds, taking deep controlling breaths as his fingers bit into the tender flesh of her shoulders.

'Alex, I think I should go back to the States,' she told him in a trembling voice.

His lids were lifted, his eyes narrowed. 'You're homesick? The visit from your parents has made you aware that you miss it more than you realised?'

She shook her head. 'I love it here. I—I just think I should go.'

'Why?' he demanded abruptly.

She avoided his gaze. 'I just—I can't——' she moistened her lips. 'I don't think I can——'

'Make love with me any more,' he finished grimly, throwing back the bedcovers to begin pulling on his clothes. 'That's it, isn't it? When it comes down to cold facts you don't want me near you, do you?'

Morgan flinched at the contempt in his voice. 'Alex, I——'

'Do you?' he bit out between gritted teeth.

She swallowed hard. 'No,' she admitted miserably.

Alex drew in a ragged breath, still for a moment, and then he was dressing more speedily, his expression harsh as he pulled on his jacket. 'That's what I thought. I tried to tell myself you were different, and your eagerness to make love these last months seemed to prove that,' his mouth twisted. 'You just wanted your hold over me to be all the stronger, didn't you?' he accused contemptuously. 'God, you're a better actress than I gave you credit for—you acted the willing lover so well——'

'I *was* willing.' She sat up, her expression pleading.

He halted at the door. 'Was, in the past tense,' he dismissed angrily. 'Well, I'm not as hooked as you thought I was, Morgan. I want you, yes, I could probably even make love to you now if you asked me to, but *I'll* never ask you again. You'll never make me plead and beg for your body.'

'Alex!' she cried as he opened the door. 'Where are you going?'

'Out! I can't bear to be near you, Morgan.' His mouth twisted. 'You're everything I thought you weren't, every foul name a tease like you can be called. Well, I watched a decent and proud man controlled and manipulated all his life by his desire for one woman's body; I'm not about to fall into the same trap myself!'

'Alex . . .?'

'Your timing is all wrong, Morgan,' he told her vehemently. 'Another few months and maybe, just maybe, I might have been so captivated by you that I fell into that trap. But not yet.'

'Alex, don't leave like this!' She swung her legs to the floor, intending to go to him. 'Let's talk. I'll explain——'

'I'm not interested in explanations,' he scorned. 'I don't need them now.'

'But you can't go out!'

'Why not? It's only eleven o'clock. And I know several women who would be glad to give me a bed for the night. Pleasant dreams, Morgan,' he taunted before leaving the room, the sound of his car leaving the house seconds later telling her that he had indeed gone.

CHAPTER TEN

MORGAN sat on the side of the bed for several stunned minutes, just staring at the closed door. Alex had gone to another woman. And she had forced him into it.

But surely he wouldn't really go to another woman's bed? It would be a betrayal of all they had shared. And hadn't she betrayed the marriage vows she had made to him, the agreement she had made with him, by refusing to make love with him? If he went to another woman tonight it would be her own fault.

She kept thinking he would come home, that his anger would cool and he would come back and they would talk. But the hours passed and there was no sign of him, no powerful engine in the driveway to tell of his return, just an empty silence. As empty as the rest of her life was going to be without him . . .

She had been a fool, she knew that now; she had known it the moment Alex walked out of the door. He hadn't had an affair with Glenna, he was too honourable a man for that. He might have found Glenna attractive, might even have wanted to make love to *her* because of her similarity to her sister, but he would never have made love to his brother's wife. Courtney was not his child.

She groaned low in her throat, convinced now that she had misjudged Alex in the worst way possible. She should have known this as soon as Janet Fairchild told the lie, should have known her husband well enough to believe in him. And now he had gone to another woman, convinced that she no longer wanted him, that her enjoyment of their lovemaking had been a sham, a way of trapping him into some sort of physical tie to her, the same tie his friend had known. He might not be trapped, but she was, knew that she would never leave him, never.

He hadn't returned by morning, and dressing Courtney in warm clothes she drove out to see her mother-in-law. She could hardly telephone Rita and ask if Alex had spent the night there! This way the visit would look like a casual one; she and Courtney often went over to see Rita in the day now, declaring a truce for Courtney's sake.

After half an hour Rita hadn't so much as mentioned Alex, and her own casual mentions of him received only a normal response. Alex hadn't spent the night here.

'Would you mind taking care of Courtney for a while?' Morgan asked her mother-in-law. 'I have some shopping to do, and he's only just got over a fever.'

Rita smiled. 'You know I'll love to have him. Leave him here any time you want to.'

Morgan drove to Janet's house, her anger burning to a fury. She shouldn't have listened to the other woman's spiteful words of accusation, but that didn't excuse Janet's need to say them in the first place. She would put an end to this vindictiveness once and for all.

Janet seemed surprised to see her when she was shown into the lounge, putting her magazine down to stand up slowly. 'Have you come to say goodbye?' she taunted.

'No,' Morgan told her abruptly.

'No?' She raised dark brows. 'Then you have less pride than I thought.'

'Less sense, you mean,' Morgan retorted angrily. 'For even listening to you. I don't know why you did it, what you hoped to achieve, but I've come here to call you a liar—a vicious, vindictive liar!'

The other woman looked unruffled. 'Is that what

Alex told you?' she drawled.

'Alex hasn't told me anything,' she snapped, 'because I haven't bothered him with this.'

'Then maybe you should.'

'Why? So that he can be disgusted I would even listen to such lies?' Morgan derided.

Janet flushed. 'If it's the truth——'

'You know it isn't,' she shook her head. 'Alex is hard, cynical, but he's also totally honest. He would never have touched Glenna.'

'No?'

'No!' Morgan was breathing hard in her anger. 'I'll only say this once, Janet, and you'd better listen. I don't ever want these filthy lies repeated to anyone else, and if they are you'll regret it!'

'Are you threatening me?' Janet scorned.

'You'd better believe it! I just hope you haven't already ruined my marriage to Alex.'

'And what are you threatening me with?' Janet derided.

'I believe your husband and children love you very much,' Morgan said softly, seeing how the other woman blanched. 'Think what it would do to them to know how bitter and twisted you are inside.'

'Get out!' Janet hissed fiercely. 'Just get out!'

'I'm going,' Morgan said calmly. 'But I hope you take note of this warning. I have no idea why you feel the need to destroy other people's happiness, but bitterness like yours should be controlled or it will take over your whole life. Think about it, Janet, and treasure what you have—a husband and two beautiful children.'

Janet didn't answer her, but she knew by her pale face that her point had gone home. She just hoped it worked! Rita's dislike had been just that, pure and simple, but Janet's feelings of resentment went much further—destructively so; she could even need professional help.

But settling the problem of Janet's lies hadn't helped her find Alex, and the fact that he had been with another woman all night became a stronger possibility by the minute.

She stopped off at the shops and bought a few things for Courtney before going back to her mother-in-law's, remembering that she was supposed to be shopping; she doubted if either Janet or herself relished the idea of their conversation of this morning becoming known to anyone but themselves.

Courtney was asleep when she got back to Rita's, so she carried him straight out to the car, anxious to get home in case there had been any word from Alex, making her hasty excuses to her mother-in-law after thanking her for taking care of Courtney.

There hadn't been so much as a telephone call from Alex when she got back, and her heart sank. Where *was* he!

She carried out the normal routine of her day as if by instinct, taking care of Courtney, instructing Mrs Whitney on the menus for the rest of the week, subconsciously wondering if she would still be around to eat the food. After last night she doubted it.

She lay down herself while Courtney had his afternoon nap, and the next thing she knew it was mid-afternoon—and she was no longer alone in the bedroom! She had drawn the curtains before she went to sleep, but even in the gloom of the room she could clearly see a figure in the bedroom chair. Alex!

She struggled to sit up, suddenly wide awake. 'You came back,' she said huskily, uncertainly.

He moved slightly in the chair, his eyes gleaming in the darkness. 'Yes,' he answered abruptly. 'It is my home, after all. Would you like me to ring Mrs Whitney for some tea?'

Her tongue was cleaved to the roof of her mouth, but she knew the dryness owed nothing to thirst. She could hardly believe Alex was here. And although he still seemed distant, he no longer appeared to be angry. 'No, thank you,' she refused gruffly. 'Alex, I think we should talk——'

'I quite agree.' He stood up to switch on the bedside lamp, the room instantly bathed in a golden glow. 'And I think it had better be now.'

If she had been tired from her sleepless night Alex looked doubly so, with deep lines etched into his face, his mouth a forbidding line. 'The baby——'

'Downstairs with Mrs Whitney,' he dismissed abruptly, and sat beside her on the bed, looking down at her with dark eyes. 'I'm so angry with you I should strangle you!' he ground out.

Morgan swallowed hard. 'I know. And I'm sorry. I have no excuse for the way I've been behaving. I——'

'No excuse?' he repeated grimly. '*No excuse!*' he repeated fiercely.

'No,' she shook her head, grasping his arms so that he shouldn't leave her, quivering just from the feel of his warmth. 'I can't explain why I've been acting the way I have, I just—I want you to know I'm over it now, and—and if you'll forgive me I would very much like to be your complete wife again.' She looked at him anxiously, searching for some sign of softening towards her in that hard face. There was none.

His eyes were narrowed to icy slits. 'Why can't you explain? Don't you think I'm owed an explanation?'

'God *yes*,' she groaned. 'But I can't give you one.'

'Why not?'

'I just can't!'

'You little fool!' He shook her, his eyes glittering dangerously. 'How can you still protect her after the harm she tried to do to us?'

Morgan stiffened, her eyes widening at the fierceness of his expression. 'Wh-What do you mean?' she quivered, this time with uncertainty.

He sighed. 'Janet came to see me,' he told her flatly. 'She told me all that she'd taunted you with— everything.' He stood up, moving away from her.

She swung her legs to the floor and sat up to look at him anxiously. 'Janet came to see you?' she repeated dazedly. 'How did she know where you were?' she frowned.

'I wasn't too difficult to find,' he derided. 'I'm usually at my office at two o'clock on a Wednesday afternoon.'

'Your office . . .' she choked weakly. 'I never thought to look for you there.'

Alex looked at her sharply. 'Why would you look for me at all? You wanted to leave, remember?'

She swallowed convulsively. Janet had told him everything, and he was so disgusted with her for believing such lies about him that he couldn't bear her around any more.

'I think your sister is ill.' She didn't answer his question.

'I know that now,' he nodded. 'And so, thank God, does she.'

'She does?' Morgan frowned.

'Yes,' he sighed, his hands thrust into his trouser pockets. 'She didn't come to see me to cause more trouble, Morgan, she came to try and make right a serious wrong. Whatever you said to her this morning certainly brought her to her senses. She's going to seek professional help.'

'But why is she like that?' She tried to delay the inevitable, that of having Alex ask her to leave his life.

'Janet isn't the only one to blame for the way she is—we all are. Oh, not you,' he dismissed. 'You weren't even here when it happened. It's the rest of us that have been so damned insensitive,' he bit out grimly. 'You see, eighteen months ago Janet lost a baby. She hadn't realised she was pregnant, and she continued with the hectic pace of her life as usual. By the time she realised what had happened it was too late. She lost the baby at only three months—a little boy,' he finished softly.

Tears filled Morgan's eyes at the suffering Janet had kept hidden from everyone, the agony of losing a baby.

Alex seemed not to notice her tears but continued talking. 'Of course we all expressed sympathy, the sort of inane remarks that everyone spouts at such a time, nothing that really meant very much, or eased her pain. Then Glenna became pregnant,' he said harshly. 'Everyone was overjoyed by the news, and Janet's loss was forgotten. Can you imagine what it did to her, to see Glenna growing with a healthy child, to see the attention she was getting, and know that some of it should have been hers?'

'Yes,' Morgan choked. 'Oh, poor Janet!' She had never dreamt that such heartache was the reason for Janet's need to cause others pain.

'Yes,' he agreed dully. 'I think when Glenna died, and you became Courtney's mother, her hate passed on to you.'

'Will she—will she be all right?'

'I think so,' Alex nodded. 'With professional help and a damned sight more thoughtfulness from her family. Now we come to the lie she told you about Glenna and me.'

She chewed on her bottom lip at the chill that came into his eyes. 'I was a fool, I knew that as soon as you left last night. Glenna was married to your brother.'

'But she was unhappy here.'

'Not that unhappy!'

'No,' he acknowledged tautly. 'Although you've probably guessed, from your own experience with her, that my mother made Glenna's life here almost unbearable?'

'That much was obvious!'

He sighed. 'Mark was my mother's baby, no woman would have been good enough for him. She chose to believe what she wanted to, never seeming to realise how deeply Glenna and Mark loved each other.'

'Then Courtney wasn't a way of keeping the marriage together?'

'Something else one of the charming members of my family implied?' Alex derided almost disbelievingly. 'No, Courtney was a wanted and loved baby, a result of their love for each other. But how did you feel about him when you thought he was my son?'

Morgan frowned. 'I loved him, the same as I always have.'

'And me? How did you feel about me?' He seemed tensed as if for a blow.

Honesty—she had to give him honesty. 'The thought of you and Glenna—I hated it,' she told him heatedly. 'And I hated you for making me her substitute——'

'Dear God, you thought that?' he groaned.

'Yes,' she admitted miserably. 'And it tore me apart. I knew you didn't love me, but I thought what we did have was for me, not—not—I was a fool,' she repeated shakily.

'And what do we have, Morgan?' Alex asked softly. 'A good relationship in bed?'

'Definitely that. And—and my love for you,' she faced him fearlessly. 'I love you, Alex,' she told him strongly. 'I loved you before I married you, and I've loved you ever since.'

For a moment he seemed not to want to look at her, he was so deep in thought, then he gave a ragged sigh. 'Your honesty has always—shaken me,' his eyes glowed deeply grey as he looked at her. 'It isn't something I'm used to in women.'

'I'm sorry you were hurt in the past,' she said with

gentle sincerity. 'But I would never use my body to blackmail our relationship. This other woman——'

'My mother,' he told her harshly. 'I watched her control and manipulate my father from the time I knew what was going on. God, what a family you and Glenna both married into!' he said disgustedly. 'My mother, who used her body to control her marriage, my sister, who's more deeply scarred inside than any of us realised, my brother, who never quite grew up, and—and an emotional cripple.' He looked at her with pained eyes. 'The last one is me,' he admitted raggedly.

'Alex . . .?' She was shocked by what he had just told her. There hadn't been another woman who had hurt him, only his mother, and the friend she had thought he was talking about yesterday had been his father! Somehow she couldn't see his mother in the role he had painted for her.

'Oh, it's true, Morgan,' he seemed to read her thoughts. 'Even her children were produced with precise regularity, at four-yearly intervals. My father worshipped the ground she walked on, and she used that, she used it to control him!'

'Maybe she loved him too, Alex,' she comforted him. 'After all, she's been a widow for some time——'

'Twenty years,' he confirmed.

'And she never remarried. It can't have been easy bringing up three children on her own, even when she sent you all to boarding school. Wouldn't it have been easier for her to remarry? She's still an attractive woman; she must have been beautiful then.'

'She was,' he nodded. 'And maybe she did love him, in her own way. But it was a destructive love, not the sort of love I wanted for myself. When we married, on our wedding night, and all the nights after that, when you gave yourself to me so completely, I knew you loved me. And I was afraid of that love, afraid of what it might do to me.'

'Love can't hurt you, Alex,' she told him throatily. 'Only hate and loneliness can do that.'

He closed his eyes, breathing deeply. 'When I realised you loved me I think I did hate you for a while.'

'Alex!' she gasped her hurt.

He turned to look at her, his mouth twisted into a wry smile. 'You haven't heard why I hated you yet. Knowing, guessing, how you felt, made me examine my own feelings for you. And I didn't like what I found,' he admitted hardly. 'I think it started that day we arrived back in England together and you expressed concern for how tired I looked, and told me to rest. Everyone else seemed to think I could go on indefinitely, that I could accept the deaths of my brother and Glenna as if I didn't give a damn. Only you seemed to see that I was as deeply affected as the rest of you.'

'You hid it well, Alex,' Morgan said huskily. 'You know that at first I thought you were very cold-blooded about it too.'

'I felt guilty,' he rasped. 'There'd been one hell of a row before they left. You see, they weren't coming back here, they were going to stay in the States. Glenna was becoming increasingly unhappy here, and Mark had no idea how to break away from the family. I arranged for him to run the branch of Hammond Industries in the States. When my mother found out she was furious—with all of us,' he added grimly. 'It was far from a pleasant parting for them.'

'But I'm sure they were happy to just get away.'

'I'm sure they were too,' Alex nodded. 'But I still couldn't help my feelings of guilt. Maybe if I hadn't arranged for them to leave they wouldn't have been on that plane, they would still have been alive. Then you came back here with me, and I couldn't seem to stop the desire I felt for you. I told myself it could only be desire. But instead of having the affair with you that I wanted I asked you to marry me. I had no idea why I'd done that.'

'Courtney——'

'Had nothing to do with it,' he shook his head. 'The situation could have been resolved by my moving to the States—I didn't need to marry you. No, I wanted you, but I just didn't want to have to admit that I did. Then after we were married there seemed no reason to admit anything; we were happy together without my having to make any kind of emotional commitment. When you suddenly turned against me three days ago I didn't know what to do. I didn't understand it, and I couldn't seem to stop it either. So instead I walked out.'

'Last night——'

'Spent on the couch in my office,' he admitted grimly. 'Both times I've walked out on you, last night and the day we came back from our honeymoon, I've spent there.'

'You should have just come home,' Morgan choked.

'I couldn't. I was still afraid of what I might have to do to get you to stay, to remain my wife.' Alex swallowed hard, looking very pale. 'I still can't say it, damn it!' he ground out harshly. 'Even though I may lose you if I don't.'

Morgan stood up to run to him, her arms about his waist as she pressed her head against his chest. 'You won't lose me, and you don't have to say anything, Alex. I don't need the words,' she smiled up at him tearfully. 'I can say it for both of us; I love you, Alex. I love you so much.'

His arms closed about her fiercely. 'You deserve the words,' he spoke roughly into her hair.

'But I don't *need* them.' She kissed the hard line of his jaw, knowing this man was truly hers, that he always had been. 'All I need is you.'

'I need you too, Morgan,' he groaned. 'Without you now I think I'd die!'

'Darling . . .' she raised her face to his, kissing him with all the love inside her. 'Come to bed, Alex,' she invited breathlessly. 'Come to bed and let me love you.'

And as they made love Alex told her the words she longed to hear, told her over and over again until they became one being, one person, drowning in that love.

He grinned down at her a long time later. 'I feel—free,' he said lightheartedly. 'For the first time in years I don't feel a need to hide the way I feel. And it's all due to you, my darling.' His arms tightened about her. 'I've said it before, and I don't think I'll ever stop saying it—you're one hell of a woman, Morgan Hammond.'

'And you're one hell of a man, Alex Hammond,' she laughed up at him happily, sobering suddenly. 'Alex, I have something to confess to you.' She played with the dark hair on his chest.

'Confess away,' he invited indulgently.

She drew in a deep ragged breath. 'When Janet told me—what she did, I—I—There were special circumstances why I *think* I believed her so readily.'

His brows rose. 'There were?'

'Mm.' She chewed on her top lip, unable to meet his gaze. 'I've been a little emotional lately, and——'

'A little!' he scorned.

'Well, there's a reason for it!' She gave him an indignant look. 'I had something I was going to share with you, to share with everyone at Courtney's christening—if Janet hadn't spoilt it with her lie.'

'I had some cake, thank you,' he taunted her.

'Alex, will you please be serious!' she said crossly.

He did his best to keep a straight face. 'Of course. But can I tell you one more time that I love you first?'

'Never stop telling me that.' She kissed him deeply,

knowing by the gleam in his eyes as she raised her head that his desire had been aroused once again. 'Alex, I—I——'

'Well, spit it out, woman,' he growled, nuzzling into her neck. 'I have three nights of abstinence to make up for.'

'Well, make the most of it now, buster,' she snapped, 'because in a few months I'll be so fat you won't be able to get near me!' She watched as he slowly raised his head, passion and amusement both gone now as he looked from her face to her still flat stomach, lingering there, his hand moving to frame the slight swell he had detected. 'I know it doesn't look much at the moment,' she giggled at his awe-struck expression. 'But another month or two and your daughter will be kicking about like a soccer player.'

'Football,' he corrected. 'It's called football over here,' he explained at her puzzled look.

Morgan gave an angry snort. 'Is that all you have to say about your child?'

'How do you know it's going to be a daughter?' he teased, desire rekindling in the depths of his eyes.

She gave him a haughty look. 'Because I've decided it is, that's why. Another boy and I would be outnumbered by the Hammond men three to one— and that's no fair contest for any woman.'

'*You* could handle it,' Alex assured her softly. 'You could handle a whole army of us—with your love and fierceness.'

She swallowed hard, knowing how privileged she was to have his trust, his love. 'How do you really feel about the baby?'

'I love it. I love *you*. I love the whole damned world!'

'Just me is enough for this moment.' She pulled him down to her. 'I'm a very demanding woman.'

Alex laughed throatily. 'You certainly are—thank God! I never knew I had such strong sexual urges until I met you.'

'I know,' she teased. 'And after telling me you'd keep them to a minimum too!'

'Wanton!'

'Sex-maniac!'

'*Love*-maniac,' he corrected huskily, suddenly serious. 'I love you so much, Morgan. I want nothing more than to take care of you and our children. After all, Courtney will need more than one sister to spoil.'

'He certainly will,' she agreed softly, before all the teasing stopped and the serious loving began.

Harlequin ® Plus

LOVE SUPERSTITIONS

Many of us who are single may sometimes wish for a crystal ball to tell our futures—especially in the area of love. Failing that, there are a number of little incidents that are said to prophesy what the future holds. We are not suggesting that these things have any real basis in fact, of course, but just for fun you might like to know of a few. If you find that one comes true for you, we'd be delighted to hear about it!

If a cat washes its face in front of a group of people, then looks at you, you will be the first in the group to marry.

You know that the man you love will propose if a white pigeon lands on your doorstep.

If a white speck appears on your little fingernail, then be prepared for a new love.

You will be married before the year is out if you *accidentally* step on a cat's tail.

If you want to sneeze but cannot, it means that someone loves you but is afraid to confess his feelings.

If your forefinger and little finger can touch over the back of your middle finger, you may marry anyone you choose.

Enter a uniquely exciting new world with

Harlequin American Romance™

Harlequin American Romances are the first romances to explore today's love relationships. These compelling novels reach into the hearts and minds of women across America... probing the most intimate moments of romance, love and desire.

You'll follow romantic heroines and irresistible men as they boldly face confusing choices. Career first, love later? Love without marriage? Long-distance relationships? All the experiences that make love real are captured in the tender, loving pages of **Harlequin American Romances.**

What makes American women so different when it comes to love? Find out with **Harlequin American Romance!**

Send for your introductory FREE book now!

Get this book FREE!

Mail to:
Harlequin Reader Service
In the U.S.
2504 West Southern Avenue
Tempe, AZ 85282

In Canada
649 Ontario Street
Stratford, Ontario N5A 6W2

YES! I want to be one of the first to discover
Harlequin American Romance. Send me FREE and without
obligation *Twice in a Lifetime.* If you do not hear from me after I
have examined my FREE book, please send me the 4 new
Harlequin American Romances each month as soon as they
come off the presses. I understand that I will be billed only $2.25
for each book (total $9.00). There are no shipping or handling
charges. There is no minimum number of books that I have to
purchase. In fact, I may cancel this arrangement at any time.
Twice in a Lifetime is mine to keep as a FREE gift, even if I do not
buy any additional books.

Name _____ (please print)

Address _____ Apt. no.

City _____ State/Prov. _____ Zip/Postal Code

Signature (If under 18, parent or guardian must sign.)

What romance fans say about Harlequin...

"...scintillating, heartwarming...
a very important, integral part of mass-
market literature."
—J.G.,* San Antonio, Texas

"...it is a pleasure to escape behind a
Harlequin and go on a trip to a faraway
country."
—B.J.M., Flint, Michigan

"Their wonderfully depicted settings make
each and every one a joy to read."
—H.B., Jonesboro, Arkansas

*Names available on request.

Begin a long love affair with

SUPERROMANCE.

Accept LOVE BEYOND DESIRE, **FREE.**

Complete and mail the coupon below, today!

- -

FREE! Mail to: SUPERROMANCE

In the U.S.
1440 South Priest Drive
Tempe, AZ 85281

In Canada
649 Ontario St.
Stratford, Ontario N5A 6W2

YES, please send me FREE and without any obligation, my
SUPERROMANCE novel, LOVE BEYOND DESIRE. If you do not hear
from me after I have examined my FREE book, please send me the
4 new **SUPERROMANCE** books every month as soon as they come
off the press. I understand that I will be billed only $2.50 for each book
(total $10.00). There are no shipping and handling or any other hidden
charges. There is no minimum number of books that I have to
purchase. In fact, I may cancel this arrangement at any time.
LOVE BEYOND DESIRE is mine to keep as a FREE gift, even if
I do not buy any additional books.

NAME _____ (Please Print)

ADDRESS _____ APT. NO.

CITY _____

STATE/PROV. _____ ZIP/POSTAL CODE _____

SIGNATURE (If under 18, parent or guardian must sign.)

This offer is limited to one order per household and not valid to present
subscribers. Prices subject to change without notice.
Offer expires March 31, 1984   134 BPS KAFG